PSYCHIC LIES

SAMANTHA BELL

PSYCHIC LIES

SAMANTHA BELL

CHAPTER ONE

Bianca. I've been looking for you.

Listen to me. I have something important to tell you.

No, I'm not losing you again.

Bianca! Come with me.

The woman's petite form radiated power. She wore a blank white mask that covered her entire face. Her hair was long and black, just like her dress. She hovered in the air, her bare feet just an inch from the floor. A crystal necklace dangled from her neck, swaying back and forth as she hovered in place.

The masked woman raised her hand and clenched her fist. All around us, the metal and wood began to tremble, then buckled under the force until it splintered and twisted. A cable against the wall snapped with a twang and the ground shook beneath my feet.

Join me and I'll show you what real power is!

I gasped, jolted out of my nightmare by my alarm clock. I slammed my fist down on the snooze button, rolling over and cursing my early morning classes. I still hadn't adjusted to waking up before the sun.

I hid under the covers and sulked for another five minutes before the snooze alarm went off. I surrendered, slapping the clock once more and sitting up.

Over the past month, I had managed to make my dorm room a little bit more personalized. I had a photo of my family on my dresser; it was my favorite photo, the last picture that all four of us took before my abuela passed away last year. I added a pink fuzzy throw blanket to add a pop of color to the bedding and several strings of fairy lights framed my window. It wasn't much, but it was something. After all, I was on a limited budget and students of the Psychic Academy weren't allowed to hold part-time jobs either. I decided next time I went home I would gather up a few more things to decorate my dorm room.

Next week I would see my parents again. I had been on a teleportation ban since the teleportation incident in July. The administration decided that I was too much of a risk to leave the grounds until A: my powers were better controlled and B: they captured whoever it was that was after me.

I called my mother often, but it wasn't the same. My parents had been brainwashed to think I was at a college out of state, so I couldn't really talk to her about anything at a deeper level. With no resolution in sight, I begged Major Griffiths for a supervised visit, which he finally agreed to. A girl's tears could work wonders on even the most hardened war veteran.

I dragged myself out of bed, dressed in my black training gear and brushed my hair. Breakfast was a communal affair, so there was no way I would drag myself downstairs in my pajamas. The Major said that these early starts would build discipline, but I was pretty sure he was just biased from his military days.

While waiting for the elevator, I ran into Phylicia. Her long braids had changed from red to an ombre design of purple roots flowing to silver tips. She went out nearly every weekend and always had new clothes, new hair, or new nails to show off. Her family was rich, but they weren't on good terms, so her parents tried to buy her love with a platinum credit card. I was no therapist, but I guessed that it wasn't working so well.

"Good morning," Phylicia said.

"Morning," I mumbled, semi-coherently.

Phylicia laughed. "Still not an early bird, huh?"

I shook my head.

The elevator chimed and the doors opened. A few people I didn't talk to were in there. I ignored them as Phylicia and I squeezed in. Phylicia was tall and built like an athlete, but her physique didn't take away from her feminine beauty. I felt short and scrawny standing beside her, even after a month of rigorous training.

The elevator doors slid open and I filed out with the rest of the students, making my way across the grounds to the main building. The weather was already hot and humid; it was going to be a miserable August day. At least I didn't have to run across the path in ankle-deep snow yet — Michigan winters sucked big time.

I stuck close to Phylicia. I had never been good at making friends and after everything that happened last month, no one wanted to get close to me. It seemed that I had been labeled as one of the outcasts. I fit in perfectly with Phylicia, the only pyrokinetic student on campus, and Katie, the tiny girl who had uncontrollable visions of death and despair.

I chose cheesy breakfast burritos and my standard giant mug of coffee for breakfast.

Phylicia shook her head. "You know, you should drink more water."

"I enjoy being in a perpetual state of dehydration," I sniffed as I sat down.

Phylicia grinned and rolled her eyes. "Girl, I'm just looking out for you." She poked her fork around the slightly over-cooked tofu scramble in front of her.

"I know, I appreciate it," I said, taking a long sip of coffee anyways. The breakfast buffet always had interesting flavored creams; I chose vanilla this morning.

After breakfast I had ethics class. The teacher that replaced Turner was no where near as sexy or engaging (quite the opposite, actually) but at least he wasn't involved in a secret plan to kidnap me. He was about my dad's age, with a thin build and monotone voice. He single-handedly turned ethics into the most boring class imaginable.

My only saving grace was that Luke took this class with me. He flashed me a smile as I walked in the classroom. He was at his usual spot near the back. I took a seat beside him, slapping my notebook down on the desk as I sank into the chair.

"Good morning, sunshine." Luke's smile was enough to brighten anyone's day. His short curly hair was freshly cut with a faded design at the base of his neck. He was dressed in standard black training clothes; our uniforms were functional so we could go from sitting in class to kicking butt in the gym without having to change. His honey brown eyes lit up when I smiled back at him.

"You seem extra peppy this morning," I said. Luke was the living definition of a morning person, but he was glowing more than usual today.

"Yep, I just got some good news."

"What?"

"Ms. Blackwell is coming back today. The doctors cleared her to return to work." Luke beamed.

My mouth fell open. Ms. Blackwell had been in a coma only a week before. When she awoke, her testaments were crucial in getting Turner locked away where he belonged. I heard the gossip that her powers were too weak to teach. There was even talk that she might not ever be able to use her powers again. Of course, these were only whispers that I heard in the common rooms, so I had tried my best to tell myself that it wasn't true.

Slowly, my expression turned into a smile. "That's great!"

Luke nodded. "Yeah, I didn't believe it at first but it's true." Luke admired Ms. Blackwell — she was an extremely talented psychic, who was gifted in both telekinetics and teleportation. She trained me in telekinetics when I first arrived and she helped Luke hone is skills in longer distance teleportation, both of which had been instrumental in our defeat of Turner.

Thinking of Professor Turner always made my heart twist in a way that I couldn't explain. He had trained me in Ms. Blackwell's absence, and made me stronger than I ever could have imagined. Ms. Blackwell preached control and poise, while he only focused on brute strength. It was his training that allowed me to defeat him in the end.

I arrived in the training room after lunch as I normally did. Since the incident, I hadn't had anyone to train with one on one; I had been working every afternoon on my own.

I used my energy to pick up plates and other objects, raising them to the ceiling and setting them back down. I had taught myself how to tie knots in ropes using nothing but my mind. If being attacked by Rogues had thought me anything, it was that I needed to perfect my skills before they had a chance to come after me again.

I braced myself and used my energy to grab a ball from the floor. I slammed it down and caught it mid-bounce. It was as if an invisible giant was dribbling a basketball up and down the room. The bounces echoed in the small training area; I could hear other students practicing through the thin accordion walls that divided the enormous training facility into manageable sections.

"Excellent job!"

I heard clapping from behind me. I dropped the ball as I looked towards the voice. The basketball rolled to the feet of Ms. Blackwell.

Choking back a gasp, I spoke. "Ms. Blackwell! You're back."

The teacher smiled. Her dark hair was slicked back in a perfect bun. Her professional black dress was flawless and her boots clicked on the hardwood floor. She looked about a million times better than she did last time I saw her unconscious and hooked up to machines in a special hospital ward meant for psychic injuries.

"Good afternoon, Miss Bianca. I see that you've managed to learn quite a bit while I was away." Even her voice was sophisticated and controlled. She kept her hands clasped behind her back.

I beamed with her compliment. To further prove her point, I grabbed the basketball with a flick of my wrist and guided it back with the other training tools. "Thank you."

"I heard that Professor Turner trained you in my absence." Her voice darkened.

I suppressed a shiver and nodded.

"Hm," Ms. Blackwell paused for a moment. "Come with me, won't you?" She gestured to the door.

I followed her out of the training facility and into the courtyard. The sun was beaming down, but the brightness was obstructed by the protective forcefield that covered the entire academy. One day I'd figure out how all that stuff worked, but right now powers like that seemed beyond my comprehension.

Ms. Blackwell sat on a bench and motioned for me to join her. "I wanted to talk to you away from the listening ears of other students." She said.

We were alone in the courtyard. No one was wandering around between classes. "What is it?" I asked.

The teacher took a moment to collect her thoughts before she spoke. "Bianca, what happened with Turner was disastrous. We're only lucky that he didn't succeed." Her eyes met mine. "I fear that whatever he was up to isn't over and whoever he was partnered with will strike again."

Goosebumps rose up my arms. I had never seen her so deathly serious before, and serious seemed to be her default emotion.

"He tried to kill me. He tried to kidnap you," Ms Blackwell said. "I heard that your only saving grace was the skills he taught you. Ironic." Her lips twitched with a shadow of a smile. "But, if they do strike again, as I fear they will, you will need to be ready."

I nodded. "I've been training every day."

"I've heard that as well. I met with Luke earlier today." Ms. Blackwell paused. "Bianca, I am not the sort of woman who thinks that anyone should have to hide behind a man, but when it comes to this, I would feel better if you surrounded yourself with strong psychics until those Rogues are captured."

I nodded.

"Therefore, I asked Luke and Ryland to keep a close eye on you."

I blushed and turned my burning face away from her. How much did she know about my relationship with them? Luke and Ryland were the star pupils of the academy. "I see."

"Just temporarily." She added. "Luke will escort you to and from classes in the morning and Ryland will do the same in the afternoon. Major Griffiths agreed to it."

Did I get any say in this? Being with both of them would only complicate my feelings further. I wanted both of them, though I had been forcing myself to stay with Luke. Ryland's mood swings were exhausting.

I understood my teacher's concern so I agreed half-heartedly, wondering how in the hell would I manage this sexy-boy-sandwich that I had been assigned to.

CHAPTER TWO

"Good morning, sunshine," Luke greeted me with his perfect grin.

Day one of constant supervision. I had almost forgot until I opened the door to find Luke waiting for me.

Luke pushed off the door frame and shoved his hands in his pockets. He had his backpack slung over one shoulder. His stature oozed sex appeal.

I almost felt my self control slip through my fingers. Since that night in his bedroom, I hadn't let myself be alone with him again. Seeing him brought back memories of is hard body against mine, the way he kissed every inch of my body, touching all of my most precious places. He had treated me like a queen, and I had run scared.

I told myself that now was not the time to be looking for love. Simple physical pleasure should be the last thing on my mind right now. Not when there was a bunch of Rogues out to get me. After that night with Luke, I swore that I would keep my eyes on the prize. Once the academy was safe again, I would re-open my heart.

"Good morning," I said with false energy.

"You're beautiful as always," Luke added.

I looked away, adjusting my ponytail awkwardly. "Come on, let's get to the dining hall before all the coffee is gone."

∞

"So I heard you get to go visit your folks next week?" Luke asked.

I looked up from my lunch and nodded.

We were sitting together at the far end of the cafeteria. The morning had gone off without a hitch, seeing how we had our first class together anyway. Luke dropped me off at my second class (Abnormal Sciences, yuck! Even in this place I hated science class.) and met me at the door as soon as the bell rang. It was like having my own personal body guard.

I didn't miss the looks people shot us as they walked past. They were probably wondering why the star student of Psychic Academy was risking his neck to protect a dangerous nobody. I did my best to ignore their glares.

Luke probably didn't even notice, as he was taking his instructions to not take his eyes off me quite literally.

"I'm really looking forward to see my parents," I said after taking a sip of water. I was trying to take some of Phylicia's advice to heart.

"Hey, I'm here for the Princess." A figure stopped at the edge of the table.

I looked up. Ryland. He was standing at the end of the table with his arms crossed over his chest. His icy blue eyes froze my soul. He did not look happy to have been put on Bianca-watching-duty. I wasn't sure if his scowl was permanent or not — this guy had some serious resting bitch face.

I forced a smile. "Hi, Ryland."

"Are you done eating? I need to drop you off at training before my afternoon class, and I'd really rather not be late."

I wilted under his glare. "Yeah, ok." I grumbled and pushed back in my chair with a little too much force. As I stood, the chair fell backwards with a bang. About a hundred pairs of eyes stared at me and I bit back a frustrated sigh. "Come on, let's go."

Luke exchanged a glance with Ryland, but didn't get up. Maybe he was glad to be rid of me. He had babysat me all morning, after all.

I hated this.

I followed Ryland to the training area, staring at the floor as we walked. Ever since the night of the incident, he had changed. That night he was so supportive, kind, and impressed by my skills. Now he was cold and aloof. Had I done something to offend him? I had to find out.

We stopped at the door of the training facility. The courtyard was empty and quiet.

"Hey, Ryland?" I said softly.

"What?" The sharpness of his voice cut into my skin.

"I was wondering if maybe you'd like to get together after class or something." My voice faded away shyly.

Ryland scoffed. "We will be together after class if you didn't notice. I'm in charge of protecting your ass until the end of the day."

Any confidence remaining was dashed out. I didn't bother trying again. "Ok, then." I mumbled. "I guess I'll see you after." Ryland was silent as I pulled open the heavy facility door. I didn't look back as the door clanged behind me.

The training facility had been opened up into larger portions for group training. I looked around, walking past a group of teleporting students. They vanished and reappeared on marks etched onto the floor.

I found my group one section over. I recognized the three students from the last time I had embarrassed myself during Turner's lesson. These kids were much more experienced than me. I had proved myself in my eyes, I knew I was powerful, but they still looked down their noses at me.

Ms. Blackwell was there, watching them warm up. She was looking even better than yesterday. She was standing a little straighter in her stiletto-heel boots. How she had returned from a near-fatal injury as still maintained her fashion sense was beyond me. How did she train in those things anyway?

Ms. Blackwell turned to me as I pulled the accordion divider shut. I was the last to arrive, despite being early. Everyone must have been excited to get back to training with the best telekinetic teacher on campus.

The only one of the students I knew the name of was Qadir; he was the one who humiliated me in front of Turner and the other students. I lost control of my powers and he taunted me for it. I couldn't let that happen again. I couldn't embarrass myself when Ms. Blackwell was watching. If there was anyone in this academy that really, truly cared about me, I'd like to think that it was her.

I put on a strong face and joined my classmates.

"Everyone, please welcome Bianca Hernandez. I don't believe you've met?" Ms. Blackwell asked.

Qadir snickered. "Oh, we've met."

"I joined a group session while you were away," I said to her as neutrally as possible. "But, I am very excited to show how much I have improved since then." I shot a glare a Qadir, who shrugged.

"Excellent." Ms. Blackwell broke us off into pairs.

Thank goodness I was with someone who wasn't Qadir. I had seen her in the cafeteria once or twice before, but I didn't know her name. Whoever she was, she did not look happy to be paired with me.

I forced a diplomatic smile. "Hi, I'm Bianca."

"Gracie. Let's just get this over with." She muttered.

Her expression told me everything: I was the cursed new girl and anyone who got too close to me was at risk. I was an outcast. Shunned by the very people who were supposed to understand me. If other psychics were scared of me, what hope did I have in the real world? I swallowed my pride and nodded.

Ms. Blackwell gave us drills to perform. Simple ones like passing a ball back and forth with our energy and then moving up to heavier objects. This went on for half an hour and just before I died of boredom, she clapped her hands to get our attention. "Break time. Take five and then we'll continue."

I sighed and let the metal plate slowly sink to the floor. It was hard to believe that only a month ago I found simple psychic exercises like this to be exhausting. I used to faint every time I used my powers, now I was able to work for a few hours and only get dizzy or hungry. It was like my teachers promised, I would get better with time and I had. But it seemed that I was the only one who was impressed with that. I mentally patted myself on the back before grabbing my water bottle and sinking down onto the mat to stretch.

"So, new girl." Qadir's voice rang in my ears.

I glanced up. "What?"

Qadir's smirk warped into a frown. "No need to be rude, I was just saying hi."

If he never spoke to me again, it would be too soon.

"I was actually hoping we would get paired together today," He went on.

"Why?" I asked. "So you could humiliate me again?"

Qadir scoffed and shook his head. "I never did anything. You being all loose with your powers is what caused that. Seriously, you need to get a hold of yourself before you hurt someone."

I knew he was just trying to get under my skin. I took a long drink of water to avoid saying something I'd regret. "Whatever." I said, hoping he'd take the hint and leave.

"So, you wanna try me again?" He raised his eyebrows.

I wasn't sure if he was flirting or being serious, but either way I was not interested. I'd rather go on a date with Major Griffiths before I even looked at Qadir again. "No thanks." My voice was clipped.

Qadir didn't get the hint. "Why not? I thought you said you got better?" He waved his hand and my water bottle trembled and then flew out of my hand.

"Hey!" I jumped to my feet. "Give that back, Qadir."

"Or what?" He sneered.

The other classmates looked over. Ms. Blackwell had still not returned from her break.

My cheeks went hot when I realized everyone was watching us. "Give back my bottle," I said. "I don't feel like messing around today." I clenched my fist.

"Oh," Qadir faked a frightened shiver. "I'm so scared of you, Bianca. I bet you'd love to kick my ass."

I gritted my teeth. "Oh you know it, too bad it won't happen."

"Yeah, 'cause you can't!" He sneered.

My patience snapped. I lunched forward, summoning all of my psychic energy. The tingle ran up my spine and to the base of my skull. The energy surged and grabbed my opponent. I pulled the bottle hard and sent it flying across the room.

Qadir gasped under my strength. "Fuck, let me go!" He grunted.

"I thought you wanted me to kick your ass? Did you not just challenge me?" I lifted my hand and squeezed him tighter.

Qadir finally fought back. I felt his energy pulse against mine and he managed to get free. He might have been an annoying asshole, but he was skilled.

I stepped back and raised my arms, fighting with my energy against his.

With a flick of his wrist, he sent the rubber balls stacked against the wall flying towards me.

I broke off and jumped back to avoid them. "Is that all you got?" I challenged him.

Qadir laughed and motioned for the other students to step back. "You're serious then, aren't you? Ok, don't say I didn't warn you." He raised a ten-pound metal plate into the air.

Metal was quickly becoming my specialty. I motioned with my fingers, feeling the pulse of energy move from my brain down through my arm, and snatched it away from him. With a groan, the metal twisted and buckled under my invisible psychic strength.

Qadir's mouth fell open in shock. "Holy shit, where'd you learn that."

"Somethings aren't learned in a classroom." Before I thought better of it, I swung my arm and sent the twisted metal disk straight at him.

Qadir dodged, throwing up his arm and sending the plate away. It spun off towards our watching classmates and collided with Gracie. She gasped as the metal hit her in the gut and she sank to the floor with a groan.

"BIANCA HERNANDEZ! QADIR TOMA!" Ms. Blackwell shouted from the doorway. She teleported to Gracie's side. She was unconscious, but she looked to be alright. There didn't seem to be any visible damage.

But internal bleeding was still a possibility. I wasn't a doctor, but I guessed she'd be alright.

I let my energy fade and my hands fell to my sides. "Ms. Blackwell! It was an accident!"

"She started it!" Qadir's voice was shrill.

One of the students ran off to get medical help. The others stared at me in stunned silence.

"It wasn't me. It was —" My protests died in my throat as Ms. Blackwell shook her head in disappointment.

∞

"I am very surprised at you, Miss Hernandez."

I slouched in my chair. How many times had I been in the Major's office since enrolling here? It had to be at least twice a week at this point. I knew his secretary by name and I noticed when his desk had been rearranged.

"I'm sorry, sir," I said. "But it wasn't all my fault. If you'd listen to my side of the story."

The Major cut me off with a wave of his hand. "It doesn't matter whose fault it is. What matters is that your classmate is currently in the hospital with two broken ribs. We're lucky the damage wasn't worse."

"I didn't throw the plate at her!" I sighed. I was tired of everyone not believing me.

"I thought you were ready to train with the others, but it's obvious that you can't control your powers as well as we thought." Major Griffiths continued. "I understand that there was a disagreement, and Qadir will also be punished, but injuring another student is a serious problem."

I nodded. There was no fight left in me anymore. Why bother trying to defend my actions when no one bothered to listen. It was obvious that I had been written off as a bad egg since the incident last month. Maybe I was bad luck after all.

"In light of this event, we have decided to further suspend your home visits."

My jaw dropped. "What? No! I haven't seen my parents in months!"

The Major shook his head. "Young psychics who cannot control their powers or their emotions," He added with a look. "Are a danger to the community at large. We cannot allow off site visits until you can control yourself."

I collapsed back in my chair. This wasn't a school. It was a prison.

CHAPTER THREE

It felt as if something had been torn out of me. Seeing my parents was the last shred of light that I had been holding onto since the academy went on lock-down. Now it seemed so hopeless.

Ryland was waiting for me outside the office, still upholding his Bianca babysitting duty. "What happened?" He asked. "I went to your training to pick you up and someone said there had been an accident." He sounded genuinely worried.

"I don't want to talk about it," I said. "I screwed up again. That's all."

"Talking might help," Ryland said.

I couldn't believe my ears. Ryland, who had just shunned me hours before, was suddenly caring about my feelings again. His hot and cold attitude was too much for me to handle right now. "I just want to go home." I said.

"You mean the dorms?"

I cringed inwardly. No, I meant home. But that wasn't an option now. "Yeah, that." I agreed.

"You should have dinner." Ryland said as we walked towards the exit closest to the dormitories.

"I'm not hungry." I said flatly.

Ryland didn't press the matter further. He walked me to my dorm room and shrugged awkwardly. "Well, if you need me, I'll be around." He said.

I forced myself to look at him. "Thanks, Ryland. Really. I just need to be alone right now." I looked away as I shut and locked the door.

The room was dark and dreary. The white walls seemed so cold to me now. I curled up on my bed and let myself cry, biting my pillow so no one in the hall could hear me.

∞

The sound of my phone ringing woke me from a troubled sleep. Despite my hazy mind, I had a feeling that it was important, so I reached out and answered in a groggy voice. "Hello?"

"Bianca!" It was Daniel.

I bolted up from my bed. "Daniel!" I cried. "Oh my gosh, you have no idea how good it is to hear your voice. What's up? Is everything ok?"

"Yeah, everything is fine. I wanted to check it and see if you needed anything for your visit on the weekend." Daniel said. His cheery voice broke my heart.

"Oh," I sank back down onto the mattress. "Yeah, about that. I guess I'm not coming anymore."

"What?" He gasped.

"Something happened during training," I said, keeping the details vague. "And apparently I'm not trustworthy enough to be around normal people. My powers are too erratic. Someone might get hurt." I rolled my eyes.

There was silence on the other end of the line. "Oh, I see." Daniel said finally. I could feel the hurt in his voice. "I was hoping we could go to the beach or something, like we always did in the summer. Before people move away for college."

My heart strained in my chest and my eyes swam with tears. "Yeah, me too." I sniffed. The lake wasn't the nicest beach, but anything would be better than this place. I hadn't realized how much I was looking forward to visiting until it had been snatched away.

"They can't keep you there forever, right?" Daniel said after a moment. "I mean, it's not a prison."

"It's starting to feel like one," I said darkly. I forced myself to put on a brave face and keep my tone light. "But don't worry. I'm sure they'll let me visit soon. And, when they do, we can go to the beach and get ice cream and do anything you want." I hoped it wasn't a lie.

"Yeah." Daniel didn't sound convinced. "Oh!" He added. "There was something else I wanted to tell you too."

"What is it?" I could sense the juicy gossip.

Daniel lowered his voice. "I overheard my dad talking to someone yesterday night. Something about work." The way he stressed the word work dropped a hint that it was about the psychic division of the FBI. His father was an inspector and even his son didn't know much about what went on there. "He mentioned something about needing extra security for something. He mentioned the academy."

I was silent in shock.

"Anyway," Daniel said. "Not sure what it's about, but something might be happening soon. Maybe that's why they're on high alert. I'll let you know if I get wind of anything else, but Dad is pretty good at hiding his tracks."

"Ok, thanks." I said. I didn't want the conversation to end. Talking to Daniel made me feel like I was home again. I hadn't seen him since I was torn away from him and put into the back of a unmarked police car, destined to be sent back to Psychic Academy.

I talked with Daniel for over an hour and it broke my heart when he had to go. I hung up the phone and let the silence settle in around me. It was heavy and thick with feeling. I felt so closed off from the world. So alone and lost.

A knock on my door snapped me out of my pity party.

"Who is it?" I called, not wanting to get out of the comfort of my bed.

"It's me." Ryland.

"I'm fine. Don't need babysitting, thanks."

"I brought you dinner."

It was then that I noticed how hungry I was. I hesitated for a second before abandoning my pride and opening the door with a flick of my wrist. The door swung open and I didn't have to leave my bed. (Talk about a win-win.)

Ryland's eyes lit up, seeming slightly impressed with my use of psychic energy for everyday tasks. In his hand he had a styrofoam container of food from the cafeteria. The smell of noodles and stir-fried veggies filled my small room.

Ryland walked in and passed me the food before taking a seat at my desk. "Thought you'd be hungry."

"Starving." I admitted and closed my door with another snap of my fingers. I dug into the meal, not caring that Ryland was watching me eat like a crazy person. We were all aware of the strain that our psychic powers had on our bodies and the need for food was almost constant.

Ryland was silent while I ate, his eyes drifting around my room slowly and then stopping on the photo of my family. It looked like he wanted to say something, but was holding back.

I swallowed the last of the noodles and threw the empty container in the garbage bin under my desk. "Thanks," I said.

Ryland gave me a soft smile. "No problem. I am supposed to be looking out for you after all."

I looked down at my hands, running my fingers against the blanket on my lap. "Yeah. Sorry about that." I wasn't sure why I was apologizing, but it was the least I could do.

"Not your fault. I'm just doing it because Ms. Blackwell and the Major asked me to."

I looked up. "I don't need a bodyguard," I said. "I told her that. We can call it off."

Ryland shook his head. "How can you say that when that masked woman is still at large?"

I blinked, taken aback.

Ryland stared at me for a second and then sighed. "They didn't tell you?"

"Didn't tell me what?"

"That the masked woman who attacked us that night and her two cronies are still out there. Rogues are still running rampant in this city and we have no idea who they are."

My mouth went dry and fear prickled through my body. "No, she didn't say that."

Ryland shook his head. "Typical. Why do they do this shit? Withholding information never helps someone who's at risk."

"At risk?" I repeated.

"They think she's going to come after you again." Ryland explained.

"I can take care of myself."

Ryland chuckled darkly. "Really? Against her? You know that's not true. All three of us didn't stand a chance against her and she escaped Federal agents."

Ryland was right, but the truth hurt anyways. "So that's why they're keeping me here?" I whispered. "This isn't about my powers at all. Or my parents."

"Well that incident with Qadir was a good reason to keep you here, but no, there's more to it than that."

I wasn't surprised that the whole campus knew about my fight with Qadir, but juvenile gossip was the least of my worries now. My chest ached as the anxiety spread through me. I was in much more danger than I originally thought.

Ryland waited a beat before speaking. "Hey, it's going to be ok."

I looked at him, refusing to cry in front of him. "Thank you."

"For what?" Ryland raised his eyebrows. "If anything I just added more stress."

"No," I insisted. "Thank you for telling me the truth. It's more than anyone else has done for me here."

Ryland nodded slowly. "I guess it's because I sort of know how you feel."

My eyes met his icy blue gaze. "Really?" I found that hard to believe. He was so good at everything. Maybe a bit of a loner, but it seemed that he liked it that way. He wasn't easy to get close to. He was like a well-sharpened blade that you could feel the cut before you even touched it.

"Really," He said. "I wasn't exactly welcomed here with open arms. I'm sorry I was so cold to you these past few weeks, but that Rogue incident really set me back."

I was silent, waiting for him to continue.

Ryland sighed and leaned forward in the chair. "You see, when I came here, it wasn't by choice. A kid that I was training with back in Cali got lost in limbo for a bit, showed up in Europe a few days later. I didn't exactly have a clean record, so I got blamed for it. I swear I never meant to screw up his teleportation, he just had a weak mind. But it didn't matter to the administration. I got expelled and transferred here."

"Oh." What could I say? I guess he did sort of understand what it was like to walk around with an invisible target on your back. He knew what it felt like for people to be afraid of being around him. No wonder Luke was the only person who sparred with him. He was probably the only psychic student powerful enough to match him.

"Don't worry about me, Bianca." Ryland shrugged. "I think I'll have to just accept that I will never be welcome back in the West Campus."

"I'm sorry if I added to your troubles," I said.

Ryland shrugged again. "Seriously, don't worry. You save my ass that night. You literally saved my life and I've been acting like a dick to you. I'm the one who should be sorry."

I reached out and put my hand on his knee, feeling the need to be close to him. "Well, how about we both just say we're sorry."

Ryland chuckled. "Let me make it up to you?"

I didn't miss the flicker of heat behind his eyes. "How?" I asked, tipping my head like a total flirt.

"Date night. Tomorrow. Me and you."

My body had been craving another amazing make-out session, but I supposed date night was a better place to start. We had never done anything with each other besides fight and kiss. Maybe it was time to give him a chance. What was the worst that could happen?

CHAPTER FOUR

Apparently, date night to a guy like Ryland meant sparring. But what else were we going to do while stuck on campus? It wasn't like we could just go out for dinner and a movie like regular teenagers.

"So, this is your idea of a date, huh?" I couldn't help myself.

Ryland looked over his shoulder and smirked. "I thought we could both use a little therapeutic anger release." He resumed pulling training stuff from a storage closet. He had closed off the retractable walls to give us a small but adequate amount of space and privacy to train together.

It was past dinner and the training room was empty on a Friday. Most of the students, who weren't been held hostage here, went home to visit their parents. Luke had forgone visiting for my sake, saying his duty was to protect me until he was told otherwise. I felt too guilty to tell him about my date with Ryland tonight.

I watched Ryland pull out the mats, noticing how his muscles flexed under his tight t-shirt. He sparred bare foot, his muscular body in training clothes that left nothing to the imagination. I fidgeted, trying to get myself to focus on the task at hand, but all I wanted was him.

"Ready?" Ryland swept back his blond hair from his eyes.

I nodded.

Ryland walked to the center of the mat. "I figured that with all this weird stuff going on and us needing to burn off some energy, I'd teach you a little hand-to-hand combat."

My physical fighting skills were severely lacking compared to my psychic skills. I had the strength of a kid and my fitness levels weren't exactly stellar. I had been working out on my own in the student's private gym, and while I had seen some progress, I knew it wasn't enough to take down a kidnapper or Rogue.

The thought of combat with Ryland sent warmth blossoming through my body. I pulled my hair into a ponytail and joined him on the large blue mat. "Ok, I'm ready."

Ryland didn't give a warning before he lunged at me, throwing his fists at my face.

I screamed and dodged, stretching out my hands and wrapping him in my psychic energy.

Ryland was frozen where he stood, caught in my invisible grasp. He grunted against the force.

I released him and let my hands fall to my sides.

"No telekinesis." Ryland rolled his shoulders and took a step back. "You can't always count on your powers, Bianca. You need to be able to fight."

I knew he was referencing the fact that for some reason he couldn't read my mind. It was like fog to him and neither of us knew why. His telepathic powers were some of the strongest in the academy, but to him my mind was dark.

I set my jaw and nodded. "Ok, no powers." I agreed.

Ryland took up a fighting stance again. "Don't run away, either. Just dodge my punches. I'll go easy on you."

I held up my hands in a defensive pose and waited for him to strike. My psychic energy pulsed at the base of my skull, but I ignored it. I had to do this the old-fashioned way.

We went for several rounds. It was obvious he was going easy on me, but after a while I actually began to anticipate his moves and dodge more successfully. I rolled away from him and blocked his attacks with considerable ease.

I help up a finger to ask for a break and Ryland put his hands on his hips while he waited for me. I collapsed on the mat with my water bottle.

"Good work, so far." Ryland said, watching me take a long drink of water. "Honestly, I didn't think you'd be able to block me as well as you have."

I screwed the cap on my water bottle and smiled. "Well, I have had a little bit of practice."

"Next, I think you should come at me."

I blinked, looking up at him from the mat.

"Your defense it pretty good, but your offensive moves need a lot of work. We'll do the same thing, but I'll block you." Ryland explained.

"I don't want to hurt you," I said.

Ryland scoffed. "No offense, but I doubt you'd be able to land a hit on me anyways."

I accepted the challenge with a grin. "Fine, let's find out, shall we?" I kicked out with my legs, but to my surprise, Ryland leaped away from them. His reflexes were better than a cat's. My mouth fell open.

"See?" Ryland laughed. "Try again."

That impossibly sexy boy had lit a fire in my competitive spirit. I would not allow myself to be humiliated. I had to land at least one hit on him, or I'd never live it down. I jumped to my feet and lunged at him.

Ryland sidestepped my attack. "You need to think before you act. I can't read your mind anyways, so don't make snap decisions. You need to calculate your every move, not run around like a crazy person."

I paused to catch my breath. From what I had observed, there was no discernible pattern to how Ryland dodged moves. It was the same when he sparred with Luke. He was unpredictable and I had no idea how to anticipate which way he would feign to get the upper hand.

My eyes caught his for a moment and I was trapped in the icy blue depths. A shiver ran through my body. I blinked. I had to focus. This was not the time to be hypnotized by a handsome face. I needed to prove myself to him.

I cleared my mind and focused on what needed to be done. I had to land at least one hit. That was the objective. If I could do that against the academy's strongest fighter, then that would be something to be proud of.

Ryland was silent and tense, waiting for me to attack.

I sucked in a breath and then came forward, jabbing with both hands.

Ryland grabbed my right fist and twisted me away, pulling me to his chest. "Nice try."

I looked up at him. We were too close. My body was against his and my hands were locked in his grip. I couldn't escape unless he let me. No, that was weak thinking. I still had a chance. He was distracted by the feeling of our bodies together too and I used it to my advantage. I twisted around and used his weight against him, sending us both crashing to the mat.

Ryland let out a gasp as he fell on his back. "Wow!" He seemed as surprised at my success as I was.

Never in my life did I think I could toss a tall, muscular guy with my tiny frame, but I did it anyways and without the help of my psychic power! I let out an excited squeal. "I did it!" It was only then that I noticed I was still on top of him.

Ryland's chest was heaving as he caught his breath. He looked at me with a warmth in his eyes that I had never seen before. "That was pretty awesome." He said. He sat up and wrapped his arms around my waist, crushing his lips into mine.

I melted at his touch. The heat that was spreading through me ignited into a wildfire as I let the sexual tension take over. I had been craving his kiss more than anything.

Ryland groaned as he pulled me against him, holding me as if he were afraid I would vanish if he loosened his grip even a fraction. He pulled away from our kiss, trailing his lips down my neck and whispering into my ear. "I want you, Bianca. Please, don't make me wait anymore."

I whimpered. My voice was soft, barely audible when I replied. "I want you too."

Ryland rolled over, pinning me between the mat and his hard body. He kissed me, running his hands down my body and cupping my breasts in his hands.

My nipples hardened against the thin sports bra I was wearing. I arched my back as he explored my body. We had come so close to this so many times, and now we would both get what we desired. My thighs trembled as he moved his hands lower.

"You're beautiful," Ryland said. He gently pulled my thank top up and my bra down, revealing my small but perky breasts. He grinned and began to tease me with his tongue.

I moaned. I as much as I wanted his touch, I needed more. I wanted him. All of him. Right here and now. I slipped my hands down my leggings, pulling them down over my hips. "Please, Ryland."

If Ryland was surprised at my boldness, it didn't show. He moved his mouth down my body until he found his prize.

I gasped and moaned as he worked me up to a climax. It took only a flick of his tongue to send me over the edge. "More, more." I begged.

Ryland put my legs over his shoulders and lowered down to me. I could feel his hardness at my opening, waiting to be thrust in completely. His eyes were fiery and his breath was hard against my skin. With one solid motion, he pushed himself into me, his large manhood stretching me to the limit.

I cried out in surprise, the pain faded quickly to pleasure. "Oh my god, Ryland." I moaned.

Ryland's breath caught in his throat as he bore down on me. "Bianca, you're so tight." He gritted his teeth as he pumped faster and faster.

Here I was being taken by him in the middle of the training room. It felt so naughty but so right. I didn't care in that moment. All I wanted was him. I held my legs to my chest and watched him reposition before plunging inside me again.

His thumb brushed against my sensitive nub, sending another wave of ecstasy through my body. Ryland groaned, pulling out and emptying his seed onto my belly before collapsing down onto the mat beside me.

I looked at him. Somehow my ponytail had come loose, and flyaway hairs were stuck to my forehead. I swept them away and let out a soft giggle.

Ryland looked at me mischievously. "Why don't we take your training to the bedroom?"

CHAPTER FIVE

The next morning, I woke up in my room with Ryland's naked body against mine. He looked like a marble statue, all hard lines and ridges of muscle. Even when he was sleeping, he couldn't lose his handsomeness.

I was shaken from my memories of last night by a knock at the door. Ryland stirred but didn't wake. I jumped from the bed and threw a t-shirt and pajama pants on quickly. "Who is it?" I called out.

"Bianca, it's me." Luke's voice came from the other side of the door. "You weren't at breakfast, I wanted to make sure everything was ok."

I froze, glancing at the clock. It was past ten o'clock, which was terribly late for students who were normally up at the crack of dawn.

"Oh, I'm fine." I replied. "Just wanted to sleep in."

Luke didn't sound convinced. "I don't want to bother you, but I need to look out for you. Can you open the door?"

I cursed under my breath and slid the lock open. I peeked out my head, making sure Ryland's sleeping form was hidden from view. "What's up?"

Luke's eyes narrowed. "Are you sure you're ok?"

I nodded. "Yep, just sleeping in, like I said. I'll come find your for lunch, ok?" My voice squeaked.

Luke didn't seem convinced, but he didn't press the matter. "Fine," He sighed. "See you later." He turned and walked away without looking back.

I sighed and shut the door softly. I rested my forehead on the frame.

"You know, you could have just told him I was here." Ryland said.

I looked up.

Ryland was sitting in bed with his hands behind his head. He looked totally relaxed and indifferent to the fact that Luke almost caught us sleeping together. "It's not like you're dating him or anything." He said.

Ryland didn't know that I had slept with Luke a few weeks ago, in a moment of weakness while trying to forget my stress. Wasn't that what just happened last night too? I shook my head. "It's complicated."

"I know you have a thing for him too, Bianca. I'm not dumb. I know we're both fighting for your interest. This sort of thing isn't uncommon with psychics. Psychic women are less common, after all," Ryland said. He stood and pulled on his clothes.

I didn't know what to say. I wasn't trying to be a rarity and I wasn't trying to be indecisive or greedy. I just wanted both of them for different reasons.

Ryland hesitated before leaving, looking at me over his shoulder. "I don't mind whatever we're calling this. Honestly. Casual is fine for now," He said. "But, sooner or later you're going to have to pick a side."

∞

I hid in my room until lunchtime and then met Luke in the cafeteria. He didn't seem happy that I had wasted half the day away, specifically the half of the day that he was supposed to be in charge of looking out for me.

I set down my plate of pasta and smiled at him. "Hey Luke, sorry about this morning."

"It's fine," He said in a tone that meant it was anything but fine.

"I needed to sleep in," I added.

"I said it's fine." Luke's voice was firmer. "I was worried about you when I didn't see you this morning. I was going to come get you earlier but I didn't want you to think I was being weird."

I reached out and touched his hand. "It's ok. I understand that you're taking this seriously and I appreciate it." I took a breath before continuing, wondering how much to say. "Ryland told me that the Rogues are still at large."

Luke sighed. "You weren't supposed to know that."

"Hiding the truth from me won't protect me. Preparing me for the worst will." I countered.

Luke nodded. "Yeah, I guess," He said. "Alright, I won't keep anymore secrets from you." His honey brown eyes met mine. "As long as you promise to do the same."

I looked down at my pasta. I didn't want to lie to him, but I supposed that not telling him about my night with Ryland wasn't exactly a lie. "Sure. Promise." I looked back up with a smile.

That seemed to appease him for now. Luke was so loving, so sweet, so kind, and it hurt me to hide anything from him. But, I had to trust my gut and right now it was telling me that I shouldn't get these two guys mixed up with my love life. We had too much to worry about right now. What was the word Ryland used? Oh, *casual*. I'd just keep things casual until I didn't need to worry about being kidnapped in the middle of the night.

Once the coast was clear and the Rogues were behind bars then I could be normal again. I could see Daniel and my parents again, too. I sighed, pushing my pasta around with my fork but not eating.

"What's up?" Luke asked. He had two finished plates in front of him. These boys sure could eat.

I looked up again. "Nothing, just really bummed out I can't see my parents."

"It's for your own good," Luke said.

"I know." I understood, but it didn't make it any less painful. I sighed and forced down some lunch. I could only manage a few bites before wanting to be sick. I pushed my plate away. "I don't feel well. I think I should head back to the dorms."

Luke stood up. "I'll take you."

"You don't have to."

Luke silenced me with a stern look. "Yes, I do. I promised Ms. Blackwell that I would."

We walked back to the dormitories in silence. When we arrived at my room, I hesitated. "Thanks for looking our for me," I said.

Luke smiled. "No problem. Seriously." He paused. "I know that Ryland has the afternoon duty, but I was wondering if you wanted to watch a movie or something in the lounge tonight? There's no need to be cooped up in your room, especially on a quiet weekend like this."

"Sure," I agreed. It wasn't like I had anything else to do. "I'm going to nap. I'll see you later." The door shut with a click.

I didn't remember when I finally slept last night, but I did know I was still exhausted. Thinking of last night with Ryland made my body warm at the smallest memory. He was amazing. I collapsed onto my bed, hugging my pillow tightly. It still smelled like Ryland.

∞

There was a knock at my door a few hours later. "Bianca, it's me. Let me in."

I opened the door to see Ryland. He was freshly showered and his hair was still wet. He must have come straight from the gym. He was oozing sex appeal and it took all of my willpower not to throw myself at him then and there.

"What's up?" I asked.

Ryland let himself in and took me in his arms. "I couldn't stop thinking about you all day. I'm so happy that I have an excuse to spend every evening with you." He growled and kissed me hard.

I melted into his kiss, parting my lips for his tongue. I moaned as he held me in his strong arms, never wanting him to let me go. I spoke when he broke off the kiss. "Me too."

Ryland grinned. "Plans for tonight?"

I faltered. "Oh, watching a movie in the lounge."

"Why? We could do that in here." Ryland grinned mischievously.

"Yeah, but I promised Luke I would."

Ryland frowned.

"You can come too," I added with a little too much pep. My voice cracked when I realized sharing me with Luke was the last thing on his mind right now.

"Yeah, no thanks." Ryland said. "But I guess I'll have to, seeing how I'm in charge of babysitting you." His expression darkened and his voice went flat. I watched his mask of indifference fall back over his face, a mere shadow of the man I had made love to last night.

"You don't have to," I fired back. "I don't need to be babysat!" I slapped my hand over my mouth, immediately regretting my tone. "Sorry, Ryland. It's just that this lock down has me under so much stress."

Ryland nodded. "As much as it hurts me to say it, I think what you need most right now is Luke."

I pulled away from him in shock. "What?"

Ryland held my hand to maintain our connection. "I mean, Luke can take you to see your parents." He looked away. "And I think that's what you need, more than anything else right now. I know you're using me to forget, and I don't mind but, you need to do what's best for you."

As much as it hurt me, it was the truth. I couldn't think straight. I was like a caged animal and no one in the administration gave a damn about my emotional wellbeing. It wasn't right to keep someone away from their family, even it if was for their supposed protection. I was eighteen, a legal adult, and I hated the power the Psychic Academy had over me.

"You're right." I edged up on my toes and kissed his cheek. "Thank you, Ryland," I said. "You know, sometimes it's like you actually can read my mind."

Ryland's mouth twitched with a smile. "I don't need telepathy to know when someone I care about needs help."

My heart burst with joy.

"I'm not going to say that I'm not jealous," Ryland said. "But, I want to do what's best for you right now." He kissed me once more. "Let's go convince Luke to teleport you out of here."

Ryland and I met Luke in the student lounge. He looked up from the book he was reading and jerked back. It was obvious he hadn't been expecting Ryland.

"Hey, Luke." I sat down beside him. "Sorry I'm late. Ryland is in charge of my protection in the evening so he decided to tag along."

Luke shot a glare at Ryland. "I don't think you need him now, I'm here. You're good." The jealousy in his voice was undeniable. He tensed up.

Ryland raised his hands in mock surrender. "I don't mean any harm, just doing as I'm told."

I touched Luke's knee so he'd look at me. "Actually, I had a better idea of what to do instead of watching a movie."

"What's that?" Luke asked. His eyes flicked back and forth between us suspiciously.

"Well," I hesitated. "I was wondering if you could take me to see my parents."

Luke jumped out of his seat. "What? With the teleportation ban? No way!"

"There isn't a school-wide ban anymore. Just on her." Ryland countered. "You're free to go and come as you please."

Luke glared at him. "Technically, yes. But if I'm caught taking her off campus, I'm screwed. In fact, we'd all be screwed."

"Then let's not get caught." I shrugged nonchalantly.

"No. No way. There is no way I'm letting the two of you convince me to teleport anywhere."

CHAPTER SIX

"I can't believe I let you two talk me into this." Luke grumbled.

The campus was dark and quiet. The air was thick and heavy with humidity; not even the slightest breeze ruffled the trees. The moon was a silver sliver in the sky. It was a perfect summer night. A great night for sneaking out.

"Are you the kind of kid that always ran away in the middle of the night?" Luke asked.

I smiled innocently. "I may be good at climbing out of windows and down trees without making a sound, if that's what you mean."

Luke sighed. "My clean record, it'll be ruined."

"So let's not get caught." I touched his shoulder. "It'll just be quick, like when you took me to see Ms. Blackwell."

Luke shushed me and nodded towards Ryland.

"I already knew about that," Ryland said lazily from behind us. "I can read your mind, remember?"

Luke gritted his teeth and walked faster. "Let's just get this over with."

We walked against the fence to the back of the property where the teleportation area was. Any teleporting off campus was strictly controlled and somehow the school would know if anyone tried to teleport in or out of a restricted zone. So much technology I didn't understand. All I knew, was that this was the only place we could get out undetected.

Security cameras combed the perimeter, but there were a few blind spots along the fence that could be exploited by students wanting to sneak out in the middle of the night. Apparently, everyone knew about it but somehow it remained a secret from the faculty.

We stopped between two lights to catch our breath and finalize the plan.

"Ok, let's go through this again," Luke said.

"You take me to my parents house. I just want to see them for a second. I can't even talk to them, because they've been brainwashed by the FBI to think I'm away at college. Just seeing them will make everything better." My chest ached thinking about it. "And then we zip back. Easy peasy."

"And I'll stay out here to keep an eye out for any trouble." Ryland added. "Just don't be gone long; I don't want to be eaten alive by mosquitoes." He leaned against the fence and pushed his hands into his pockets.

I smiled at him and turned to Luke. "Ok, ready?"

Luke sighed. "As ready as I'll ever be." He adjusted the tracker on his waistband. They were mandatory for all students with teleportation powers, day or night. "I'm going to keep this on. It might be suspicious if it's found near the teleportation area." He grabbed my hand. "I want you to think of a place near your parents house that we can teleport to without attracting attention. If we go straight to their address and I'm tracked, it will be too obvious."

I nodded and squeezed his hand. "Got it. The 7-11 a few blocks over. If anyone asks, you just had a craving for slush puppies." I pictured the convenience store in my head.

Luke closed his eyes and we teleported with a pop of pressure.

A moment later we were behind the 7-11, just left of an overflowing dumpster. An overweight raccoon saw us and scrambled away as fast as its legs could carry it.

"Ugh," I put my hand over my nose and mouth. The unpleasant feeling of teleporting paired with week-old hot dogs was not a good mix. I moved to fresh air, where Luke was waiting.

"Good to go?" He asked. His body was used to the feeling of teleportation, so it didn't seem to bother his stomach, but it did drain his energy.

I swallowed hard and nodded. "Yep."

We walked silently, with me leading the way and Luke a few steps behind for safety. Anticipation was brewing in my gut. It felt like a lifetime since I had seen my parents and it broke my heart to be away from them.

I always thought there might be something different between parents and their adopted child. They had chose me to be in their lives. They had picked me out of a crowd and decided that I was their daughter. I was proud to call them my parents.

Tears stung my eyes and I shook my head. I just needed a glimpse of them, then I would be happy.

"You ok?" Luke caught up with me.

"Yeah," I sniffed.

Luke's expression softened and he touched my shoulder gently. Crickets chirped softly in the long grass near the sidewalk. "Hey, I didn't mean to give you a hard time about coming out here," He said. "I just don't want to get into anymore shit."

I chuckled softly. "I means a lot to me."

"Bianca?"

I froze and looked up. It was Daniel. He was coming down the sidewalk with a 7-11 bag in his hand. "Daniel!"

Luke sucked in a breath beside me, but didn't attempt to stop me when I ran to my friend.

"Oh my god, Daniel. What are you doing here?" I crashed into him, enveloping him into a hug that I never wanted to let go of.

"Milk." Daniel laughed, holding up the bag. It was heavy with a carton of chocolate milk and a few bags of candy. Daniel had a sweet tooth when he was stressed. I hoped that I wasn't the cause of his stress-induced midnight snacking. Daniel's eyes slid past me and over to Luke. "What are you guys doing here? Is there a problem?"

I thanked the stars that my best friend was not only cool with the fact that I was psychic, but actually understood the world better than most normal people, because his father was psychic as well.

"I wanted to see my parents," I said and then lowered my voice. "We're not supposed to be out here."

Daniel nodded. "Ah, breaking curfew as always, I see." He shook his head and sighed. "What are we going to do with you?" We both laughed.

Luke cleared his throat. "If you don't mind, it's not just her neck that's on the line right now. We should keep moving." He gestured to the lights of the suburb. We were only about five minutes away.

I looked at Daniel. "Walk with us? For old time's sake?"

I walked ahead with Daniel, getting him to tell me all the news from our friend group that I had missed this summer. Luke stayed behind, always alert for trouble. It seemed that not much had changed in our little slice of suburbia.

"So every time I see your parents they always tell me how proud they are of you for getting into college out of state, but every time they always forget the name." Daniel cringed. "Psychic brainwashing is seriously weird. I hope it doesn't do any long-term damage."

I sighed. "Once this is all over, I'm going to tell them the truth."

We stopped outside my childhood home. My mother had planted some new flowers along the porch. The lawn and hedges were trimmed to perfection. The windows were dark. Everyone was asleep.

My heart ached in my chest as I stood before the modest house. Daniel stood beside me with his hands in his pockets. "So this is where you grew up?"

I nodded. "Yeah," I said softly.

"I grew up just down the street," Daniel added, but Luke ignored him.

"What now?" Luke asked.

I didn't know. How was I supposed to see them this late. It was past midnight; my mother and father would have gone to bed hours ago. The street was eerily quiet. I noticed then that the crickets had stopped chirping.

"Something's not right." I whispered.

Luke nodded. "I feel it too."

It was a strange pulse in my stomach. The entire world around us seemed to go silent. I immediately went on the defensive, feeling my powers uncoil and brace for an attack.

"Let's keep walking away from the houses," Luke whispered to me.

I nodded.

Daniel, who could not feel these psychic waves, had no idea what was going on. "Uh, should I just go home?"

"No, if we're being followed, we don't need to put a marker on anyone's home." Luke shrugged nonchalantly and began walking down the street as if he hadn't felt a thing.

I followed his lead, glancing around as I did. My hand brushed against Daniel's and I held it without a thought. His skin was warm against mine. I gasped and tried to pull away, but Daniel held my hand back.

"Don't worry, it's alright," He said. "Let's act natural." Daniel knew well the dangers of Rogue psychics, so there was no need to convince him to play along.

We walked around the block and then towards the old park where Daniel and I used to play as kids. It was also the site of my second Rogue psychic fight, which brought back a flood of terrified memories. The girl I was in June seemed so distant now. If only she could see what she had become.

The pulse echoed through the air again and Luke and I exchanged a look.

"It's not safe here." Luke leaned against the swing set, playing with the tracker on his waistband.

"Do you think someone from the academy followed us?" I asked.

"No. I don't know this power. It's too dark." Luke frowned.

Daniel made a nervous sound and plopped down on the grass, fidgeting with his bag of candy.

I didn't blame him for being scared, it was kind of cute actually. His down-to-earth, honest style was a nice change from all the cocky, testosterone-powered boys at the academy. "It's ok." I whispered, then turned my attention to Luke. "So what do we do?"

Luke was silent for a moment. "I was stupid to bring us out here," He sighed. "We should teleport back."

"But what about Daniel?"

Luke glanced at Daniel and sighed, pinching the bridge of his nose.

"We can't leave him alone with Rogues, especially if they're the ones who kidnapped him last time."

"Well we can't bring him to the academy either." Luke argued.

"What then?"

"Hey guys?" Daniel said.

"He won't be safe out here," I pressed.

"Guys!" Daniel shouted.

"What?" Luke and I whirled around at the same time.

Daniel's eyes were wide and round, he was pointing at something behind us. "I think we have bigger problems." His voice trembled.

I turned and my eyes went to where Daniel was pointing. It was the Rogue from the warehouse. The big man who could manipulate steel as if it were paper. His telekinetic abilities were the strongest I had ever seen, even more so than Turner. Goosebumps sprung up all over my body.

"Good evening, children," The Rogue said with a throaty chuckle. "I was wondering when I'd be seeing you again."

CHAPTER SEVEN

How many times had I been terrorized by his voice in my dreams? I lost count. Now wasn't a time for being scared. Now was a time to fight.

"Where are the others?" Luke demanded. He pushed off the metal swing set and braced for an attack.

"Just me, kiddo." The man laughed and sneered at us. He crossed his arms over his wide chest, not moving a muscle. He was like a block of cement. "I'm just as surprised to see you."

I inched closer to Luke. "What do we do?" I whispered.

"We need to get your little friend out of here so he doesn't get hurt," He replied.

"You grab him and teleport him back to my house. I'll deal with this loser until you get back." I gave him a look that showed no fear. I could handle this Rogue for a few minutes on my own. Teleportation was near-instant travel.

Luke hesitated.

"Do it," I said. I didn't wait for him to confirm; I raised my hands over my head, summoning my psychic energy and letting it flow through my spine. I ran fill tilt at the Rogue, screaming as loud as I could.

The Rogue grinned and lifted his hands. I felt his energy push against mine. He was strong, but he was slow without his teleporting girlfriend. We seemed to be equally matched.

I glanced behind me. Daniel and Luke were gone. Good. Now it was time to let my power loose. I screamed, letting the power surge forward.

The Rogue faltered mid-step. "What the —"

I let my powers flow backwards and seized the chains from the swing set, grunting as I ripped them free and sent them flying towards my enemy. Shearing through metal was a talent taught to me by that traitor professor, and I'd ensure that I'd never forget it.

The Rogue pushed against the chains as they flew towards him. He tried to dodge but was unable to. The chains wrapped around his body like a metal snake, coiling around his chest and arms.

My hands trembled, holding the chains tightly in place.

"My, my, how your stills have improved." The man wheezed as he took a breath.

"Shut up!" I hissed and pulled the chains tighter.

"Fiery little she-devil. You're just like her."

My power flickered but regained it's hold on him. "Just like who?"

"Bianca!" Daniel's father, Inspector Dolinsky, came running through the park with Luke right on his heels.

I gasped and my hold on the chains slipped.

The Rogue ripped the control away from me and escaped the chains. They fell to the ground with a clatter.

"Stop!" I shouted. I took off after him.

Luke teleported in front of the man and punched him hard in the face. The Rogue was sent to the ground. He was unconscious and his nose was bent to the side, bleeding profusely.

"Bianca, what the hell were you doing?" Mr. Dolinsky stopped beside me, grabbing my wrist. "What's going on?"

"I, I was trying to stop him." I stumbled over my words. Mr. Dolinsky looked down at me, frowning. His curly hair was messy and he was dressed in his gym clothes. His gray FBI t-shirt was stained with sweat. "Wait, how did you find me?" I glanced at Luke.

"Well, having someone teleport in my driveway just as I was getting home was the first indicator that something was amiss." Mr. Dolinsky said flatly. "I thought the academy was on a lock down."

"Only for me," I said.

My best friend's father raised his eyebrows.

I sighed and looked down. "I know I wasn't supposed to be out here. I just missed my parents so much. Daniel wasn't supposed to get involved." I curled inward, wrapping my arms around myself. When had the summer night gotten so cold? "I'm sorry."

Mr. Dolinsky shook his head. "Bianca, you're like a daughter to me. That's why I couldn't live with myself if something bad happened to you."

I nodded quietly. "You're not going to turn me in, are you?" I looked up.

Mr. Dolinsky shook his head. "I'll look away this time, but next time I'm going to have to bring it up to the authorities. Please, please, promise me you won't leave the academy until we catch these wild Rogues." He gestured to the unconscious man.

I glanced at the Rogue. The blood around his nose had gone dark and hard. I didn't have the energy to argue the fact that I had the fight handled until I got startled. Mr. Dolinsky was right, it was too dangerous out here and I would put others at risk if I got selfish again. "Ok. I promise."

Mr. Dolinsky smiled and rubbed my shoulders gently. "You'll be alright, ok?" He said. "Please leave this to the professionals."

"Is Daniel safe?" I asked.

His father nodded. "Yes, and I'll be sure that he's not out wandering alone. It's the second time these Rogues have seen his face."

I shivered. "Ok."

Luke cleared his throat. "Uh, so what are we doing about him?" He gestured to the man at his feet.

"You just get her home safe," Mr. Dolinsky said. "I'll notify the clean up crew and get him shipped off to where he belongs." He pulled his phone from his pocket. "Now get going before we attract any more trouble."

Luke grabbed my hand. "Let's go."

I nodded and felt myself tugged out of reality, spun across miles in the blink of an eye.

I stumbled and hit the ground hard as we reappeared back on campus. I collapsed onto the ground, not having the energy to save face in front of Luke or Ryland. The grass was cool against my skin.

"What happened?" Ryland ran to my side.

I was silent as Luke recounted what happened.

"We ran into her friend at the 7-11. Right as we were getting to her folks' place, there was a bag energy in air. We changed paths to get away from the houses and got cornered in the park by the Rogue guy from the warehouse. The one with telekinesis."

Ryland gasped, going tense. "Did that asshole get away again?"

Luke shook his head. "No, thankfully, one of the locals works for the FBI. Daniel's dad. Can't remember his name."

"Inspector Dolinsky." I mumbled.

"Yeah, him. The same guy who showed up to help us at the warehouse. Anyway, he took him into custody."

"You saw the FBI come?" Ryland asked.

"No, he told us to get going before they showed up. We weren't supposed to be off school grounds." Luke added.

I felt the words aimed in my direction.

"Hm," Ryland was quiet.

"What is it?" Luke asked.

"Nothing, just something doesn't seem right."

"What do you mean?"

"Don't you find it weird that the same guy was there with the same Rogue?" Ryland asked.

"Well he wasn't there; I teleported into his driveway and scared the shit out of him. We're lucky he's on our side."

"Is he on our side?" Ryland challenged.

I bolted up from the ground, anger surging through my body. "How dare you! Of course, Mr. Dolinsky is on our side." My face was only an inch from Ryland's; I could see myself reflected in his blue eyes. "I've known him since I was a little girl. He isn't one of the bad guys. He helped us!"

"And then told you to get lost before bringing in the Rogue." Ryland didn't step down, his eyes locked onto mine. "How do you know he wasn't in on it? That he didn't free him once you were gone?"

My mouth fell open. I couldn't believe what Ryland was saying. Daniel's father could never be working with the Rouges. He was the one who saved me when my powers developed. The man who had coached my little-league soccer. The man who was like a second father to me. "No way." I turned on my heel and walked off into the night.

The boys called after me, but I didn't look back as I made my way to the dormitories. The fact that they were even considering Mr. Dolinsky a enemy was beyond offensive. He had saved our asses! Ryland was too quick to point the blame, just like others had done to him.

I stomped up the stairs to my dorm room, slammed the door and locked it behind me. I threw myself down on the bed and screamed into my pillow. My body was exhausted from the teleporting and the fighting. I fell asleep almost instantly.

∞

Sunday morning, I woke up before Luke came knocking at my door. I didn't want to be babysat by anyone today. I showered, dressed in my most comfortable leggings and went to the common room to read.

It was so early that the floor was like a ghost town. The silence was so heavy that I decided to turn on the television. The 24-hour news channel was on. I went to flip to a music channel, when a headline caught my eye.

Sixteen year old girl is the third random disappearance in the Detroit Metro area in the past week. The words scrolled across the bottom of the screen. *Three teens have vanished without a trace. Police are asking anyone with information to come forward.*

"What the hell?" I increase the volume slightly.

The news was repeating last night's breaking news stories. The anchor looked somewhat worried as she spoke. "Sixteen year old Fatima Khan is the third young teen to go missing since August first. She and two other teens have no connections to each other, but the disappearances are being treated as suspicious."

The clip changed to a couple surrounded by microphones. The wife was crying.

"All we want is our little girl to come home. Fatima, if you're out there, please come home. You're not in trouble. Please come home. We're so worried." The father's voice cracked.

The screen changed again two three photos of the missing teens. "Anyone with information is being asked to come forward."

My hand was shaking so badly I nearly dropped the remote. Three teens missing in such a short amount of time? Taken without a trace? My mind immediately went to the worst case scenario: those Rogues were taking kids before their powers manifested. They were picking them off one by one, just like they had tried to do to me.

I had no proof but the feeling in my gut. I scrambled out of the lounge and went right to my room. I punched in Daniel's phone number.

The phone rang a few times before he picked up. "Hello?" His voice was groggy; it was only seven in the morning, I must have woken him.

"Daniel! Have you heard about teens disappearing?" I nearly shouted into the receiver.

"What?" Daniel paused for a second. I heard rustling as he adjusted his phone. "Who disappeared?"

"On the news, three teens have randomly vanished." I repeated. "I think it's the Rogues."

"What? How do you know?"

"I don't know, I just know?" I tried to explain my gut feeling but failed. It was like when I tried to describe other strange premonitions I used to have as a kid. I just knew.

"Bianca, you're being weird." He said. "It's probably nothing."

I was speechless. Maybe he was mad because I woke him up on a Sunday, but Daniel had always been the one by my side, even when things seemed impossible. "Maybe," I said finally. "But I want to be sure. Can you please get your dad to call me?"

"He's been out all night. He hasn't come back since Luke teleported me home." Daniel explained. "He texted me to let me know he's working, but I don't know when he'll be back."

"Oh, right." I felt a pang of guilt. "Sorry about last night," I said. "I didn't mean to get you or your dad involved. I'm really sorry."

Daniel sighed. "Bianca, you're my best friend, but you need to be more careful. If psychic agents are telling you to stay in the academy, maybe you should. For everyone's sake. Please. Don't put anyone we love in danger."

I gripped the phone tightly. "Yeah," I sighed. "You're right."

"I'll tell him you called. Promise," Daniel said. "Just promise me that you'll stay safe."

"Promise." I said. I swore to myself that I'd keep that promise this time.

CHAPTER EIGHT

"Katie, what is it like when you get a vision?"

Katie's big eyes peeked over the edge of the book she was reading. It was Harry Potter and the Goblet of Fire. The paperback looked like it had been read at least a hundred times. "Sorry, what?"

"When you have a premonition. Or a vision. Or whatever. What is it like?" I asked again.

We were sitting the the lounge. Ryland was still upholding his side of the protect-Bianca-at-all-costs bargain, but had fallen asleep in the chair next to us. Sunday nights were always quiet in the dorms.

"Well," She said slowly, setting down her book. "It's hard to explain. Sometimes it feels like I'm in a dream, other times it's like it's happening right in front of me. Other times I just know."

"Yes, *you just know*! Like that!"

Katie raised her eyebrows at me. "Why?"

"I think I felt like that earlier," I explained. "I was watching the news and I just knew."

Katie nodded slowly, tucking her long straight hair behind her ears. "The disappearing teens?" She asked.

"How did you know?"

She gave me a tiny smile. "Because I just know." She giggled.

"Huh," I sank back into the couch.

"Have you ever felt like that before?" Katie asked.

"Sometimes, but never anything big like that," I said. "Like I used to know whoever was calling before we had caller ID. Stuff like that." I shrugged.

Katie nodded. "Hm. Yeah sounds like you might have a hint of talent in that department."

"When did your powers first manifest?" I asked.

Katie was younger than most of the other students. She was tiny and quiet and kept to herself pretty much all the time. "I can't remember a time that I didn't have visions," She said. "I was always good at finding lost things and then it grew from there. When the visions became too strong and the seizures began, that's when my mother worried something might be wrong."

"Are your parents psychic?" I asked.

Katie nodded. "Yeah, but they live normal lives. Not everyone is as strong as me or you." She blushed, realizing she had been boasting about herself. "Anyways, that's why I'm here. I'd like to get a job where my psychic skills can be used to help people."

I looked out the window. My powers used to seem fairly straight forward, now I wasn't so sure. How many hidden talents were going to manifest before I understood what the hell was going on? What was I really? Who was I? Who had given these powers to me?

Not having answers was killing me.

∞

Monday, I got a call from Daniel. I had just come back from dinner and left Ryland to go change into some gym clothes.

"What's up?" I held the receiver between my shoulder and my ear as I pulled my running shoes on.

"You seem a lot better than the other day." Daniel commented. "I'm glad. I just wanted to let you know that my dad said the Rogue was safely behind bars and he wanted to apologize for giving you hell. They wouldn't have caught him if you hadn't broke curfew."

I laughed. "It all worked out, but thanks for looking out for me."

There was an awkward pause on the other end of the call. "Hey," Daniel said finally. "Bianca, seeing you made me really happy. I knew I missed you but I hadn't realized how badly I missed you until you randomly popped up again. Calling you just isn't enough."

My chest ached. "I know what you mean," I said. I had been having the same thoughts since seeing him. I had been only steps away from the people I loved, and those damn Rogues sent me back running yet again. Being away was the only way to protect them.

"Visiting is too dangerous," I said.

"You visiting me might be, why don't I come there?" Daniel asked.

My breath caught in my throat. "You can't come to the academy. They don't let anyone in who's not psychic and the clearance required is ridiculous. Your dad couldn't even come in when he dropped me off."

"They don't have to know." Daniel's voice was mischievous in a way that I had never heard before.

"What do you mean?" I asked.

"Meet me at the back fence. There's that spot you told me about. We can see each other there." Daniel and his father must have gone back there to retrieve his rust-bucket car that I had driven the night he was kidnapped. I had forgotten all about it.

"What if we get caught?"

"Let's just not get caught then, alright?"

I paused. "Ok," I said finally. Daniel might look like an innocent nerd, but he had convinced me to break the rules more times than I could count. He was the reason I was so good at climbing out of windows in the dark. The thought brought back so many memories.

"Great. I'll meet you tomorrow at midnight?" He asked.

"Sure," I said and then remembered I was supposed to be meeting Ryland at the gym. He was going to get worried if I wasn't there soon. "Ok, let's do it. But I have to go. See you soon."

I hung up, finished tying my shoes and dashed off to the student gym in the basement of the dormitory building.

The gym was small but well equipped with everything from cardio machines to free weights and yoga mats. Just being down there reminded me of my first hot kiss with Ryland, back when I saw him as nothing but a rude boy with the body of a demi-god. Some things hadn't changed, but now at least I understood why he was so cold to people.

Ryland was waiting by the door. The glass wall that lined the gym was frosted so no one could see in, but students working out could still see who was in the hall. "There you are!" He sounded almost worried. Almost; he was good at masking his emotions.

"Sorry, got caught up on a phone call." I said.

"Hm," Ryland never talked about his parents or friends back home, so I doubted he got many calls. He was dedicated to his work and nothing else. "No worries, shall we?" He opened the door for me.

There were a few students working out. I figured we wouldn't be lucky enough to be left alone at this time of night. Maybe that was for the best? I'd happily skip my session on the treadmill for another session with Ryland in the change room.

We started with a jog on the treadmill. My fitness levels were far from where I wanted them to be but they had also improved since I first enrolled. My running speed was now at a ten-minute-mile; when I started it took me eighteen minutes.

Working out next to Ryland was some sort of sick torture. He was superhuman; he ran fast, lifted heavy, had the agility of a fox, and barely broke a sweat doing it.

I hit the stop button on my treadmill.

"You good?" Ryland asked as he jogged beside me.

"I just need to catch my breath." I leaned against the screen of the treadmill and took a sip of water.

Ryland kept running. I watched him increase the speed as if it were a walk in the park. His gray t-shirt was damp and clung to his muscular torso in all the right places. I bit my lower lip; if I were a more daring girl, I kiss him right then and there.

Ryland punched the stop button a few minutes later and jumped off the treadmill. "Ok, now on to part two."

I wouldn't like my exhaustion show. I followed him with a fake smile towards the free weights. Most of the other students had cleared out now. Two guys spotting each other's squats were the only ones who remained. I felt a shiver of excitement, eager to be alone with Ryland once again.

I caught a flash of Ryland's abs as he wiped his face on the edge of his shirt and I groaned inwardly. "So, what's first coach?"

Ryland shook his head and smiled. "What am I now, your personal trainer?"

I shrugged with an innocent smile. "Worth a shot." I stretched my arms over my head and then found my usual place with the weight machines. I had decided on a circuit to do and it seemed to be working. I'd do arms and chest one day, legs and back the next. I couldn't lift much but I had definitely seen some improvement since starting to work out consistently.

Few minutes later, the last two students left the gym. I glanced over at Ryland, who was focusing on his chest presses and must have missed the sound of the door closing. I hesitated, nibbling my lip nervously. Before I could let my shyness talk me out of it, I slid off the leg press and went over to Ryland.

Ryland was breathing hard. He clenched his teeth and pushed the heavy bar up and over his head before setting it back into place. Sweat stained his shirt in a line that ran from his neck all the way down to his abs.

I didn't wait for permission, swinging my leg over and sitting on his stomach. I looked down at him with a playful smile.

Ryland raised his eyebrows. His blue eyes looked genuinely surprised for a brief second, then a fire lit behind them. "Oh, so you want this sort of training, do you?" He grinned.

I shrugged. "Maybe?" I said sweetly. "We're all alone." I let my voice trail off for him to fill in the blanks.

"Naughty girl," He chuckled. "You like the risk of getting caught, don't you?" He sat up and pulled me into his lap; I could feel his hardness pressing against my core.

"It's not that," I moaned as his lips grazed my neck. "It's just that you're so irresistible. I can't wait any longer."

"You act so innocent, but when you're with me your such a minx." Ryland grinned.

I lowered my head to kiss him. He grabbed the back of my head and shoved his tongue between my lips. I moaned into his kiss. My body was on fire. Being with Ryland felt so hot, so good, so right. It was like nothing I had ever felt before. Our bodies fit together perfectly, as if they were made for each other.

I pulled away from the kiss and nibbled his lip. "Shall we go somewhere a little more private?"

"Bedroom?" Ryland suggested.

I shook my head. "I can't wait that long."

Ryland's eyes lit up. He grabbed my hips and lifted me into his arms. He carried me to the men's change room and locked the door behind us.

The change rooms and showers were almost always empty because people preferred to change upstairs. They were always clean and bright and, although never somewhere I would have imagined making love before meeting Ryland, an excellent place for an impatient girl like me.

"I want you, Ryland." I whispered.

Ryland growled deep in his throat. He pressed me against the tiled wall and his warm body. "You do, huh?" He whispered against my ear. "Do you want me enough to beg for it?"

A shiver ran down my spine. "Yes," I breathed. "I want you. Please, don't make me wait."

"Hm, I don't know." He teased, running his hands down my curves and slipping his thumbs into the waistband of my leggings.

"Please," I said again. My lips were trembling. Somehow I was more out of breath now than I was when I was on the treadmill. My heart was pounding. "Please!" I begged.

Ryland nibbled my earlobe. "Alright, naughty girl, I'll give it to you." He spun me around and bent me over. With a rough tug he brought my leggings down over my ass and to my knees. "No panties?" He said with surprise.

"Don't you know girls like to work out commando?" I giggled.

Ryland sucked in a breath. "I do now." Without warning, he plunged his fingers deep into his prize, stretching me open and revealing my wetness. "You are so naughty." He growled. He slipped his fingers along my slit, his touches sending waves of pleasure through my body.

I looked over my shoulder, gripping the bench tightly. I watched him pull his shorts down and his massive dick sprung free. It was glistening.

We made eye contact as he pushed himself inside me with a single thrust.

I moan erupted from deep within me. I closed my eyes, my hands trembling and clinging to the bench as he withdrew slowly to tease me. I whimpered. "More, please, more!"

Ryland chuckled, grabbed my hips and pushed inside me again. This time he wasn't slow or gentle. His thrusts were quick and hard; he held onto me, pushing in to the hilt and sending a wave of pleasure through my body.

This is how I wanted it with him. Rough. Hard. Fast. Driven by an animal-like lust. My wetness was leaking down my thighs. "More!" I begged.

Ryland reached around to play with my nipples, forcing himself down on me.

I arched my back, tipping my head to kiss him. My body shuddered. I was getting close.

"Bianca, I think I'm going to," Ryland grunted. We tensed and came together, both of us forgetting ourselves and letting our shouts echo in the empty change room.

I collapsed against the bench. My legs trembling as I sank to the floor. Ryland staggered back before kneeling beside me and kissing the back of my neck. Our desperate panting was in perfect rhythm.

"You don't think anyone heard us did you?" I asked after catching my breath.

Ryland chuckled and pulled his shorts back up. "Nah. If they did, they got quite a show." He shot me a devilish grin.

I blushed, twirling my hair around my finger. "I think I should take a shower before I go back upstairs.

Ryland's grin widened. "Only if I can come too."

We stripped down and entered one of the large shower stalls. The marble ties and chrome finishes would look out of place in any other gym. I turned on the water and shut the foggy glass door behind us.

Our lips met in feverish kisses, letting the water cascade over our bodies. I moaned against his kiss and the beast within him took over. He knelt down and spread my legs, kissing my folds and gently biting my inner thigh.

I looked down at him, my breasts heaving as I tried to calm my breaths. The water rolled down my body and onto his lips. "Ryland," I whispered.

Hearing my unvoiced request, Ryland lifted me against the tiled shower wall and claimed my body for the second time that night.

CHAPTER NINE

I could barely concentrate the next day. I sat daydreaming during Ethics class instead of taking notes. I couldn't get Ryland out of my head. He was so sexy, so addictive, so perfect in every way. Ever since he had come clean with his emotions, I was finally able to understand why he used his cold bad-boy persona to protect himself and it only made me want him more.

I barely even noticed when it was time to leave; Luke had to tap me on the head to wake me from my trance. "Huh, what?" I looked up.

"Come on, I have to take you to your next class." Luke said patiently. Judging by his tone, he must have repeated himself several times by now.

"Oh, sorry." I scrambled to put my notebook back into my bag.

"What's up? You can't concentrate today," Luke said.

I blushed. I definitely could not tell him about my change room experience with Ryland. After all, I knew that Luke had feelings for me too and I was not the kind of girl who could hurt him like that. "Oh, just looking forward to tonight."

Luke raised his eyebrows. "Why?"

I glanced around the classroom to make sure we were alone. "Because I'm going to meet Daniel."

Luke stiffened and frowned. "Haven't you learned your lesson? Don't you dare ask me to teleport you anywhere."

I shook my head and cut him off. "No, no. Nothing like that. He's coming here to meet me."

Luke relaxed a fraction. "Oh, I see," He said. "Well, as long as you're careful, I suppose."

"Don't worry about me," I said with a smile. "Actually, you don't have to worry about me at all because I'm Ryland's problem after school."

Luke shook his head. He reached out and touched my hand. Our eyes met. "Bianca, do you seriously think I don't worry about you when I'm not with you? If anything, I worry about you more when I'm not by your side. He sighed. "You're headstrong and brave and beautiful and all the things that would make any guy fall head over heels for you. I just don't want you to get hurt."

I couldn't tell if he was referring to Ryland or the world in general. I touched his cheek. "Don't worry, I'm a tough girl. I won't let that happen." I smiled to reassure him. "Seriously."

Luke closed the distance between us and rubbed his hands down my arms. "Alright, if you say so."

I fell into his honey brown eyes and before I knew it, we were kissing. He tasted like mint and espresso. His arms wrapped around me and cradled me in warmth. I hadn't kissed him in what seemed like a lifetime, my stupid heart had run scared after our night together and it had hurt him. I could feel it in his body as we kissed. The way he missed me. The way my body longed for his touch.

The door knob rattled and we pulled away from each other. Luke looked down and handed me my bag. I blushed and took it from him without a word. We walked awkwardly to my next class, brushing past the students that were already filing into the lecture hall.

'Thanks for walking me. I guess I'll see you at lunch," I said.

Our good-byes were robotic and I prayed that I hadn't messed something up some how. I watched him walk down the hall and look back over his shoulder. He flashed me a smile and then disappeared.

∞

The rest of the day dragged on. I was suddenly aware of every minute that passed, counting down the seconds until I could see Daniel. It was times like this that I needed my best friend. I was confused and lonely and scared. Daniel made me feel like I was home again.

"So, shall I meet you in the gym?" Ryland asked as we walked back to the dorms.

"Oh, uh, actually I was thinking I'd skip the gym today," I said.

"Don't tell me you want to skip straight to the bedroom?" Ryland chuckled.

"No," I tipped my head and replied in a sing-song voice. "Don't tempt me like that. I actually have something I need to do."

Ryland and I stopped at the elevator. The doors opened and we walked inside, finding ourselves alone in the dimly lit confined space.

"What do you need to do that's more important than me doing you?" Ryland whispered in my ear.

I melted a little. My carnal desires would have to wait for now. "I promised Daniel I'd meet him today." I whispered, expecting the same cold response as I got from Luke, I spoke quickly. "Don't worry, he's meeting me here. I won't be in any danger."

Ryland's eyes narrowed. "Why?"

"Because he's my best friend." I shrugged. I hadn't thought I would need to defend my choice in childhood friends to a guy I had only met a few months ago. The elevator door chimed and the doors popped open.

Ryland was quiet.

I turned to look at him. "What's up?"

Ryland shook his head. "Nothing. I shouldn't stop you from seeing your friend."

We were alone in the lobby. I grabbed his hand. "But?" I prompted, knowing there was more he wanted to say.

"I can't help it. I just get so jealous at the thought of you being with someone else," He said.

I almost laughed. "Daniel and I are just friends."

Ryland didn't seem convinced.

"Seriously," I repeated. "Just friends. We go way back. He's more like a brother to me. Don't worry."

"And what about Luke?"

My eyes widened and my face turned red, giving away any excuse I could have made.

Ryland's lips pressed into a tight line. "I see." He shoved his hands in his pockets. "I know we're just casual, but it's hard for me to look the other way sometimes. I don't want you to get hurt. I want you to be happy. But, I'm a selfish guy, Bianca. I want you all to myself, even if I know there's more that you need."

I didn't know what to say, so I hugged him tightly, resting my head against his shoulder. We stood in silence for a minute. "If you're that worried about my safety, you can come with me tonight. Stand guard?"

Ryland chuckled. "And defend m'lady's honor?"

"Yeah, something like that." I grinned and kissed him on the cheek.

"And when we get back in, I'll take you back to my castle and make a real lady out of you." Ryland's lips touched my ear and I shivered.

The cold shiver gave way to a warmth that bloomed in my core at the mere thought of another night with him. "I wouldn't have it any other way."

∞

We left the dorms shortly before midnight. Ryland was obviously trying hard to not let his jealousy show, even though I had told him dozens of times that I only saw Daniel as a friend. No one else was awake at this time of night, so the walk to the back of the property was uneventful. If any cameras saw us, it would look like an innocent late-night walk.

The breeze was still warm and the air was thick with humidity. I never much liked the late summer weather, but I decided not to complain about it, knowing that a snowy Michigan winter was only a few months away. Crickets chirped and fell silent as we walked down the path that lead to the teleportation point.

Daniel was waiting at the fence when I got there. His face lit up with a bright smile.

Happiness burst through my body. I ran the last few steps up to the fence. "You made it!"

"Of course, wouldn't miss this for the world." Daniel replied. His eyes flicked back to

Ryland and he frowned. "Uh, what's he doing here?" He asked in a low voice.

"Oh," I looked over my shoulder. "A teacher has asked that I have a bodyguard at all times because of everything that's happened." I explained. "Ryland and Luke have been accompanying me everywhere, even on campus. We have to until the Rogues are captured."

'They do seem to have a sick obsession with you," Daniel said. I wasn't sure if he was talking about the boys, the teachers, or the Rogues.

"Don't mind me," Ryland said with a shrug. "I'll leave you two alone. Bianca, call out if you need anything, I'll be over there." He gestured to a small grove of trees and benches. During the day they were a popular spot to hang out, and night they looked dark and almost forbidden.

I noticed the clipped tone in his voice but didn't confront him about it. Ryland was just going to have to get used to the fact that girls could have friendships with boys that were platonic.

"What's his problem?" Daniel asked once Ryland was out of earshot.

I sighed and shook my head. "Just boy problems," I said. "I told him not to be jealous."

Daniel blinked. "Oh, so are you two…"

"Seeing each other?" I finished as he trailed off. "Kind of. I mean, I guess so. Nothing serious." I added.

"Hm," Daniel nodded. His tone had shifted. He was quieter. His excitement had been dampened.

"Anyways," I smiled, trying to brighten the mood. "It's so good to see you." I reached through the fence and held his hand tightly.

Daniel squeezed my hand. "Yeah, it is." He agreed. "I'm glad we can at least meet like this."

The metal between us made me feel like a prisoner. "Soon enough I'll be cleared to travel again."

"Don't you think it's weird?" Daniel asked. "I mean, why are you the only one who's not allowed to leave. Something isn't right. Like they're not telling you the whole story."

Daniel had always been the kind of guy who gravitated towards conspiracy theories. I laughed it off. "No, I think they're just looking out for me and my family. You saw how crazy those Rogues were. I mean, they kidnapped you!"

Daniel shrugged. "Oh, speaking of that. I overheard my dad talking earlier today."

"What happened?" I leaned in closer, as if someone might overhear us.

Daniel's palm was getting sweaty. He let go of my hand and crossed his arms. "I'm not sure. But Agent Thompson has gone missing."

"Thompson? The lady that brainwashed my parents? The one who tried to wipe your memory?" I asked. I did not like that woman. Anyone who justified their actions as "just following orders" was not a good person in my book.

"Yep, that one," Daniel said. "I didn't hear much. But my dad seems to think she's been compromised somehow. She hasn't shown up for work in a week. None of her family knows were she is. It's not like that to happen to someone, but extra suspicious because she was involved with the attempted capture of those Rogues."

"Does your dad think they're targeting people who know me?" I asked. It sounded so self-centered to even ask that. I wasn't anything special, even if the Rogues seemed to think so. There were so many talented and strong psychics, I didn't even come close to that sort of power.

"Maybe," Daniel said with a shrug. "I don't know anything besides that, but I wanted to make sure that you were aware of it, in case it leads to trouble with you."

I choked out a bitter laugh. "Remember when my biggest issue was not knowing what college to go to?"

Daniel smiled softly. "Yeah, those were the days. I'm sorry this has happened to you. I was so excited when I found out you were a psychic. It made all that research I did worthwhile. But now I see that it just destroys lives, just like it did my parents' marriage."

I leaned against the fence, wanting to be closer to him. Daniel didn't speak of the divorce often, but I knew he blamed his dad's job for it. Keeping secrets hurt more than anything, now I understood why. "Daniel," I said. "Thank you for being my friend and sticking by me. I don't know what I'd do without you."

Daniel leaned against the fence and his hand found mine again.

I wished the metal would disappear so I could hug him but holding his hand would have to do. I looked into his eyes, wishing for a moment that everything would just go back to normal. His warmth drew me in. The way his curly hair framed his face, the way his eyes softened when he looked at me. Daniel made me feel normal again. In this crazy world, Daniel was the only link I had to a regular life. He was home.

There was a magnetic pull between us that I found myself unable to escape. As I looked into his eyes, I found myself wanting to kiss him. I pressed my lips together, fighting the urge.

Daniel leaned in and I turned my head away, blinking furiously. How could I come so close to kissing my best friend? I struggled to find my voice. "Daniel, I," I said.

"It's ok," He said. "Sorry, I was letting myself get carried away. I just worry so much about you." Daniel pushed off the fence, his true emotions locked down and closed off again.

The moon was high in the sky now. How much time had passed?

"I should get going. I'd hate to get caught out here at night." Daniel said.

I nodded. "Can I see you again soon?"

Daniel smiled. "You know I'd do anything for you."

My heart ached. "Same. I just want you to be safe. Call you tomorrow?"

Daniel nodded and began to back away in the direction of his car. "Wouldn't miss it for the world."

I stood by the fence, watching him leave. We made eye contact briefly as he started his rusty car and then he drove off into the night, his tires kicking up gravel as he went. I clung to the fence until his car disappeared around the corner.

What was I thinking? I almost kissed him! Daniel. This boy I had grown up with was looking more and more like a man every day. Handsome, caring, and honest. He was everything any self-respecting girl would dream of. Marriage material even. But I had never seen him that way until tonight.

I shook my head. "Don't even think about it, Bianca," I said to myself. "The psychic world has done enough to break his heart. You don't need to do it too."

CHAPTER TEN

I had never been in the academy's auditorium before. It was small, but clean and modern with enough tiered seating for twice the number of students currently enrolled. At the front of the room there was a stage and projector screen. The staff sat near the front of the room with the rest of the space for students to gather in clusters.

I was late, having slept in after all the excitement of last night. Ryland hadn't spent the night in my bed, possibly noticing my confused mood. After all that, I barely managed to get a few hours of sleep.

I glanced around, my eyes finding Phylicia's vibrant braids easily in the crowd. She was sitting alone near the back. I squeeze through the aisle and sat down beside her.

"Good morning sleeping beauty," Phylicia teased. "Didn't think you'd make it."

I wasn't sure what I missed more: her early-bird humor or the coffee that would surely be cold by the time I got back to the cafeteria.

Major Griffiths made his way up to the podium and the buzzing conversation quieted down.

"Wouldn't miss it for the world," I whispered before turning my attention to the Major.

"Good morning students, I'm sure you're all very disappointed to be missing your first class of the day, but there is some important news I wanted to share with you all." He leaned against the podium, his hands gripping the wood tightly.

I glanced around, finding Luke. His eyes met mine, he didn't look happy that I had missed checking in with him. He took his body-guarding role very seriously. I'd have to apologize after the assembly.

"As many of you are aware, the National Competition is coming up. First years, I'm sure you're all wondering what the National Competition is."

A murmur rolled through the crowd.

"National Competition?" I whispered to Phylicia.

She nodded towards the stage silently.

"The National Competition is a exposition for all of the Psychic Academies from coast to coast. As we were the host last year, I'm sure you will be thrilled to find out who the host for this year's competition will be." The Major explained. "The National Competition is the most important time of the year for those psychics who are due to graduate. It is a time to showcase your skills. It is a time to impress potential government employers or private companies who are interested in hiring young people with your unique and valuable skills."

I couldn't believe what I was hearing. A showcase for young psychics? Was it like auditions or some sort of horrible test? I felt myself getting nervous.

Phylicia looked excited. "I've waited years for this," She said. "Finally, I can get out of here and find my place in the world!"

Other students looked equally as excited. I watched for Luke and Ryland's reaction. Both of them were wearing a poker face. They looked serious and concentrated. Typical of the best students on campus.

"Now, without further ado, I would like to announce the campus who will be hosting this year's competition." Major Griffiths looked out into the crowd. Energy buzzed in the air like static. "That campus is," He paused for dramatic effect. "West Campus, California."

The room exploded with cheering. Everyone seemed overwhelmed with the idea of traveling to the west coast. Everyone except one person.

Ryland was sitting in his seat looking ahead blankly, not even noticing the people celebrating around him. He was as still as a statue.

My heart ached for him. He should be the happiest of any of us, getting to go back to his home turf. But, now that I knew the truth about his expulsion, I wondered if he would even be allowed to compete.

The Major finished with a few more housekeeping announcements before everyone was dismissed. I sat, waiting for the rest of the students to file out so I could join Ryland. He and Luke were standing in the row, not speaking.

"You coming?" Phylicia asked. "You have time for that coffee before second period."

I shook my head. "No, I think I'll be ok for now. I need to talk to someone."

Phylicia looked over to the boys. "Still running with them, are you?" She shrugged. "Ok, have it your way. I'll save you a seat at lunch."

"Thanks," I said before shuffling through the seats to join Ryland and Luke. I could feel the tension. I put on my best smile. "So, this is exciting, isn't it?"

"I don't want to talk about it." Ryland shrugged past us and left without looking back.

My mouth fell open. I was trying to comfort him and he ran off without so much as looking at me.

"Don't worry about him, he'll be ok." Luke shrugged. "Obviously he's going through a lot right now." He rubbed his temples. The stress radiated from him. His shoulders were stiff.

I touched his shoulder gently, feeling him relax a fraction. "Why is this so important?"

"Didn't you hear the Major?" Luke asked. "Top psychic recruiters are going to be there. Government agencies, scientific researchers, military, anything, you name it. If a psychic wants to escape civilian life, this is their chance."

So, in other words, this competition was basically the SAT exam for psychics. I had never really thought about what would happen once I was trained. I had always assumed I'd go back to a normal life. Maybe some people didn't want to be ordinary. "But it's in California. He was expelled! Are they going to let him compete?"

Luke shrugged. "I don't know."

"We have to make sure they let him!" I hissed, grabbing Luke's sleeve. "He'll never forgive himself or the academy if he misses his chance."

"Ryland and I are both set to graduate soon this year." Luke's voice was even. "Yes, he should be allowed to compete, but he decided his own fate when he fucked around with a teleporting student. He could have gotten that kid killed. I wouldn't be surprised if he would never be hired."

I couldn't believe what I was hearing. Ryland and Luke were supposed to be friends, but they sure didn't act like it most of the time. "So you don't want him competing?"

"I didn't say that," Luke shot back. "We're in different categories, his attendance will have no impact on my performance."

"So we have to make sure he can compete!"

"Or maybe Ryland needs to learn his lesson. That rich kid has had it too easy. It's about time that he learn about consequences!"

I was shocked. I stepped away from Luke and shook my head. I couldn't argue with him. "Whatever." I turned on my heel and stormed out of the auditorium without looking back.

I pushed through the halls and didn't stop until I reached the Major's office. My fist was trembling, but I knocked as politely as I could.

"Hello, come in." His secretary called me in.

I opened the door and got straight to business. "I need to talk to the Major."

"I'm sorry," The secretary said, obviously flustered. "He's meeting someone right now."

"Please, it's urgent." I begged.

She shook her head. "You can sit here and wait, but he's currently in a meeting." She was interrupted by the sound of the office door being flung open.

Ryland stalked out. I had never seen him so angry before. He walked right past me, not even acknowledging me, and slammed the door behind him.

The Major stepped out next, looking just as pissed off. "Hold my calls!" He spat and shut his door again.

The secretary and I both looked at each other in shock. Whatever had happened, it wasn't good. I spun around and ran after Ryland.

"Ryland!" I called. The halls were empty now. I caught a glimpse of him turning a corner. He was on the way to the training facility. I ran after him, sprinting with a speed I had never thought I could reach before. "Ryland!"

I caught up with him in the courtyard. "Wait, Ryland."

He spun around, his icy eyes glaring at me. "Didn't I tell you to leave me alone?" He looked away, jaw flexing. "I just need to be alone."

"If this is about the competition, we can fix it," I said, trying to catch my breath.

Ryland frowned. "You can't," He said. "I know you think you can fix everything, but you can't." He put a hand on the door but didn't open it. He was fighting a war in his mind, wanting to talk to me and wanting to leave. I could see that he was arguing with himself.

I put my hand over his. "Will you at least let me try?"

Ryland closed his eyes and exhaled. There was a long pause. "How?"

I smiled. "Leave it to me."

∞

I put on my best damsel-in-distress voice. "Please, Ms. Blackwell, you have to let Ryland come with me to the National Competition.

He's been keeping me safe; how can I travel with peace of mind if he's not there?"

Ms. Blackwell considered my words for a moment. "Luke Herrington will be in attendance," She said.

Shit, I hadn't thought of that. "Yes, of course Luke is a wonderful guy, but I know that he won't be able to cover me all of the time. That's why I need Ryland to come too. The Major isn't letting him attend, but there must be some way to convince him."

Ms. Blackwell leaned back in her chair and tapped her fingernails on the armrest. "Well," She said slowly. Her eyes flicked back and forth as she thought about it. "I suppose we could make a case for him."

I sighed in relief. "If you could try, that would be great."

The teacher smiled slowly. "Bianca, you're not just asking me because you want him to compete, are you?"

I blushed and lost my nerve. "What? No! Why would I?"

Ms. Blackwell chuckled. "Because you know how important this is to him. Plus, he has a lot more personal interest with it being at his old campus." She paused. "Tell me, do you know why he was expelled?"

I nodded.

"And do you know the seriousness of his actions?"

I nodded again. "Yes, ma'am. But I also believe in second chances. I would hate it if he lost his opportunity to show his talents. Besides, once he graduates, he'll never be the Major's problem again."

Ms. Black laughed at that. A true laugh, not one of her refined snickers. "Well, you have a point there." She smiled, her face lighting up. "I'll speak to the Major on Ryland's behalf," She said. "If you promise me something."

"Of course, anything," I said.

The teacher leaned forward and lowered her voice. "Just promise me you won't attract too much attention to yourself at the National Competition. You never know who'll be watching."

Something in her tone sent a chill through my body. I nodded. "I understand."

CHAPTER ELEVEN

"Students will form two lines." Ms. Blackwell was pacing in front of us, looking more like a drill sergeant than a professor. "We will teleport in groups of two: one teleporting student to every pair. It is important that you stick with your group at all times. The teleporters have been briefed on the location of the campus, so you need not to worry."

I glanced at Ryland, who was looking ahead. "We did it," I whispered.

"I can't believe you did." He glanced down at me before returning his gaze to the front of the line.

In less than a few days, everything had been prepared for us to leave. The students with teleporting abilities that were strong enough would take us cross-country in an instant. It was no easy task for anyone, but it was the most efficient and safest way to travel.

I stood close to Ryland. He was the other half of my pair. Ms. Blackwell has single-handedly convinced the Major and the dean of the west campus to allow Ryland to compete. I thought the idea of letting him compete was much more favorable to the idea of him saying under the academy roof for another year, and I was right.

I adjusted my backpack. I wasn't sure how much stuff to bring so I brought everything I could think of. I was pretty sure I over-packed, but I'd rather be prepared.

The line shuffled forward as the groups of students began to teleport out of the campus. With over one hundred students attending, it was going to take a little while. Ms. Blackwell and some of the other teachers kept everything running like clockwork.

Soon, it was our turn.

A girl about my age was the next teleporter in line to take students. She took one look at us and her face went red. She staggered back, tapping Ms. Blackwell's shoulder. "I can't take them. He's..." She trailed off, her eyes wide.

Ryland sighed and looked away. It seemed his reputation had reached everyone.

Luke shouldered past the blond girl. "I'll take them." He said gruffly.

Ms. Blackwell nodded. "Thank you for volunteering."

Luke shrugged. "Not the first time. Won't be the last." His eyes moved from Ryland to me. "Ready?" He asked.

I nodded at the same time as Ryland. The three of us joined hands. How many times had we done this before? I let my mind go blank. The energy burst around us, teleporting us across the continent in just a few seconds with a pop.

When I opened my eyes again, I was dizzy and nauseous. I leaned against Luke for support.

Ryland groaned beside me. He hated teleporting.

"I have to go back, please stay out of trouble." Luke had to teleport many pairs of students, seeing how skilled he was. He disappeared before I could reply.

It was then that I noticed how hot the air was. It was hot and dry, the sun beaming down on us. I looked to Ryland, who had an unreadable expression on his face, and then turned around to take in my surroundings.

We were somewhere in the desert. The campus was made of square concrete buildings with tall metal walls surrounding the perimeter. It had a much more military style than the campus in Michigan. It was larger too, probably twice the size.

The students from our campus were being led to a large building that looked like a dormitory.

A man dressed in black was ushering students towards the line. "Welcome to the west campus, if you follow me, we're going to show you to your rooms."

Ryland and I joined the line, with Ryland looking down and away from all the west campus staff. He was tense and walking stiffly, like a robot.

"Hey," I grabbed his hand and gave it a reassuring squeeze. "Don't be nervous. I'm here with you."

Ryland glanced at me and his expression softened. "Thanks, Bianca. Really." He gently let go of my hand. "Let's not be too public here though, ok? I don't want you getting dragged into any drama."

I pushed down the disappointment that rose up in my throat and nodded. "I get it. No problem."

Once we arrived at the dormitory we were directed to different stairs. "Ladies to the right, men to the left." A student wearing a volunteer badge shouted out.

"I'll meet you in the lobby in an hour?" I said to Ryland, who nodded before being sent down the left hallway. I gave him a little wave before turning to the right.

A girl was standing at the mouth of the hall. "Name?" She said. She was tall with bushy brown hair and a splattering of freckles across her face.

"Bianca Hernandez."

"Room 214, near the end of the hall." She said and then motioned for the next person to approach.

I found my room unlocked. The door swung open and I was surprised to see two beds in the room. I flung my bag onto one of them and looked around. Whoever my roommate was, they weren't here yet. I hoped it was someone from my campus.

"Hey girl!"

I turned around to see Phylicia. "Phylicia! Hey, please tell me you're my roommate."

Phylicia grinned. "Yeah, it's me. They keep us with our own crowd for the most part." She had two suitcases in tow.

I glanced at her luggage. "That's a lot, we're only here for a week."

Phylicia flipped her braids over her shoulder. "Yeah, I decided to pack light." She giggled at my expression.

I glanced over at my backpack, which had been filled with only the essentials. "I guess I'm a bit of a minimalist."

Phylicia didn't respond, busy unzipping her suitcases and organizing her things. She had countless outfits, three make up bags, hair supplies, shoes, and the list went on. She hummed to herself as she unpacked.

I watched her while I unpacked my training gear, ballet flats, and a small bag of toiletries. It didn't take long, so I pulled back the curtains to get a better look at the grounds. I could see nothing but desert past the tall metal fences.

"We're in the Mojave Desert," Phylicia said. "Southern California."

"It's the middle of nowhere." I wondered aloud.

"The closest town is Lancaster, but it's a pretty boring place if you're used to the big city. This area was used for military training at one point. Now it's the largest psychic training academy in the country." Phylicia explained, sounding more like a Wikipedia article than her usual self.

"How do you know all this?" I asked.

"I did my research ahead of time. It's smart to know what you're getting into. The competition is always fierce, but the students here are something else entirely." She snapped her smaller suitcase shut and tucked it under the bed. The larger one sat propped against the wall.

"Really? What makes them so different?"

Phylicia shook her head and laughed. "You've met Ryland haven't you?" She asked sarcastically. "Just trust me, these students are as hardcore as the desert that surrounds them, and their Dean makes the Major look like a fluffy kitten. They had the most wins last year. I wouldn't doubt that they're going to go all out on home turf."

I nodded quietly. I plopped down on the bed and stretched. "Either way, I hope they feed us soon. I'm starved." I had abstained from a large breakfast, knowing how nauseous teleporting made me feel.

"Same," Phylicia said while checking her hair in the mirror. "I think I'll go explore. Want to come with?"

I perked up at the thought of getting out of this cramped dorm room. "Absolutely!" I jumped off the bed and slipped my running shoes back on. "Actually, I was supposed to meet Ryland downstairs, maybe he can give us a tour?"

"Sounds good," Phylicia said in a voice that wasn't quite sincere.

I wasn't sure what her opinion was on Ryland. She didn't seem to hate him like some of the other students and she most definitely didn't fear anyone. Maybe if she got to know him, they'd realize they had a lot more in common than they thought.

The halls were quieter now, with only a few students looking for their rooms. I didn't recognize any of them. We made eye contact but neither of us said anything. Phylicia walked with her eyes straight ahead and I followed her. If the students of the west campus were as bad ass as she said, I thought it best to stick with someone who could hold her own.

The girl with the brown hair was still standing at the end of the hall. She stepped in front of us as we tried to pass. "Where are you going?" She demanded.

Heat bristled around Phylicia. "Excuse me? I didn't think we were prisoners here."

"Tight security this year. All guests must stay in the dormitories until the opening ceremony this tonight."

Oh right, when we jumped across the continent, we had also been sent back 3 hours. No wonder I was starving.

"We weren't going outside," Phylicia lied. "We were meeting someone in the lobby."

The girl gave her a suspicious look and stepped aside. "Fine, but just remember no one is allowed out until sixteen hundred hours."

Phylicia stormed down the stairs and I followed her silently.

The lobby was still buzzing with activity as more students were ushered to their rooms. There were seating areas, several wide-screen televisions mounted on the walls, a concierge desk manned by an older woman with a tablet in her hands. I could see a door leading to a computer lab and small library, but I doubted I'd be allowed in there either.

"Bianca," Ryland's voice came from the stairs.

I looked up.

Ryland slipped between two other students and jumped the last two stairs. "Are they giving everyone a hard time or is it just me?"

"I think it's all of us." I shook my head and then remembered Phylicia was standing beside me. "Oh, this is Phylicia, have you two met?" I asked as I introduced them.

"No not formally," Ryland said. "Nice to meet you."

"Hey," Phylicia said.

"I've seen you around campus. You're the fire girl, right?"

"Pyrokinetic. Yeah, that's me." Phylicia's voice was flat.

I sensed the awkwardness building. "Anyways!" I laughed nervously. "I was hoping you could show us around."

Ryland frowned. "We're not suppose to leave the dorms," He said. "And I really don't need to draw any more negative attention to myself."

Phylicia opened her mouth to argue, but was cut off by a shout.

"Holy shit, it's him!"

We turned around to see a tall, muscular red-haired guy. He was dressed in training gear, his fiery hair pulled into a short ponytail. He was flanked by two other meat-headed jocks. "It's Ryland Williams. The prodigal son returns." The red haired guy sneered.

Ryland's jaw flexed as he clenched his teeth. He stood straight and silent, not looking away from the trio.

"Who's that?" I whispered.

Phylicia grabbed my wrist and pulled me back. "Trouble, that's who."

The smallest of the trio had shaggy blond hair and a fire burning behind his eyes. "You have some nerve showing up here after what you did to my brother." He spat.

The lobby was deathly quiet. Everyone was watching to see what would happen next.

"I'm not here for trouble," Ryland said evenly. His body was tense, ready to fight if the situation didn't diffuse immediately.

"You know how fucked up Kevin is now?" The red haired guy said, stepping into Ryland's personal space. He jabbed his finger into Ryland's chest. "I think we outta teach you a lesson."

The blond grinned and nodded. "Let me do the honors. It's my family that suffered the most." He reached out to grab Ryland by the collar of his shirt.

Ryland easily dodged and took a few steps back. "I'm not looking for trouble." He repeated, holding his hands up. "I'm here for the National Competition, that's all."

I held my breath. I had no doubt that Ryland could easily out fight these goons but getting into a fight would surely get him a one-way ticket back to Detroit and an instant disqualification from the competition.

The trio stared him down, but no one moved. It was the tensest waiting game I had ever seen. All eyes were on them, whispers began to float around the lobby.

"I'm not going to fight you," Ryland said firmly.

The blond guy twitched angrily. "You're mine!" He shouted and lunged. Suddenly he stopped as if he had been frozen in midair.

"That is enough!" Ms. Blackwell emerged through the crowd and separated the boys with a flick off her wrist. They stood still and stiff under her power. "Save the fighting for the ring, gentlemen."

The trio glared at Ryland before slinking off to the common rooms. The lobby was silent for a moment and then the whispering rose up again.

"Go on, back to your rooms," Ms. Blackwell waved everyone away.

Where was the west campus faculty? I couldn't believe that they trusted a bunch of power-hungry students to play nice in such close quarters. I breathed a sigh a relief, at least Ryland was out of danger, for now.

"I really put my neck out for you, Ryland. Please refrain from making me regret convincing the Major to let you compete." Ms. Blackwell said with a frown.

Ryland's shoulders slumped as he was released from her psychic hold. "Ms. Blackwell, I didn't start it, please believe me."

The teacher raised her hand for silence. "I know," She said. Her voice went low and cold. "But, Mr. Williams, I do expect you to finish it. Teach them a lesson that the west campus won't forget."

CHAPTER TWELVE

Our meal was served in a mess hall twice the size of the dining hall back home. The recreation building looked like an hold airplane hangar, separated into lounge areas, a media center, and the long narrow hall for communal meals. The more time I spent on campus, the more I could see why Ryland hadn't wanted to leave. Everything was immaculate and modern.

We entered two-by-two; Phylicia was to my right. Luke and Ryland were behind us. I was relieved when Luke finally came to the dormitory. He was tired and cranky from shipping all the students across the country, but he could at least intervene if Ryland's presence stirred up more trouble. Their friendship was a tangled and confusing one, but I couldn't judge, especially when I thought about my love life.

Warmth was radiating from the dining hall; it was large and simple in design. Long metal tables stood in rows, with metal benches for seating. Dinner was waiting for us in covered metal dishes.

We were ushered in by a volunteer student from the west campus. Each campus was required to sit together. West campus took up two long rows of seating, with the other three only taking up one. Thankfully, we were directed to a seat closer to the front, where a temporary stage had been erected.

Once we were seated, the east and south campuses were let in one by one. I was impressed by the discipline. Everything here went as smooth as clockwork.

My stomach cramped at the smell of food. I stared at the covered dinners, feeling more like an animal than a human. Breakfast had been hours ago and the added three hours only made my gnawing hunger worse.

Luke sat across from me and I noticed his hands were shaking.

"You ok?" I asked.

Luke met my eyes. "Exhausted. Don't worry about me." He forced a smile.

"Well I'm starving," Phylicia added. She was watching the last of the south campus walk in, drumming her fingernails on the metal tabletop. A small flame flicked across her knuckles.

Finally, once everyone was seated, a tall man in a gray suit took his place at the podium. "Good evening everyone," He said. His voice boomed, amplified by the microphone on his lapel. His eyes were cold, and his face looked like it was made out of stone. "On behalf of the Federal Psychic Academy, I am pleased to welcome you to West Campus." He gestured to the rows one by one. "If the representatives from each campus could stand for recognition?"

A woman stood up at the tables closest to the door. "Good evening. I am Dean Brier, and on behalf of the east campus, thank you for having us." She spoke with a Boston accent. She was beautiful and fit for her age and her salt-and-pepper gray hair was cut short. The east campus students wore black training uniforms with a golden stripe across the chest.

The south campus stood out the most, dressed in shades of gray and army green. A man stood up, looking a bit too young to be in charge of the second largest campus in the country. "I am Dean Freeman. On behalf of the south campus, I would like to thank you for having us here." His voice had the perfect Texan twang.

Major Griffiths stood up at the end of our table. "I am Dean Griffiths. It is my honor to be here. On behalf of the north campus, thank you." I had never heard him not use his military title before.

"And I am Tim Kennedy, Dean of the west campus for the past decade. On behalf of the west campus, welcome and make yourself at home. Thank you for attending the most anticipated event of the year." The dean said.

Kennedy snapped his fingers and rubber bracelets appeared in front of every student. "These bands will help us discern who is from where at a quick glance. They also have codes for the security system and will open any door that you are permitted to enter. While you are here, please enjoy the use of our library, media room, fitness center, or cafeteria."

"So that's his skill," Luke whispered. "Apportation."

I turned the bracelet over in my hand. It sort of looked like a fitness tracker made of bright blue rubber. There was a small bump at the center, probably where the computer chip was located. I slipped it onto my left wrist.

"After dinner, the opening ceremony will be held in the auditorium. I won't keep your from your meals any longer. Enjoy!" He stepped down from the podium. He and the other deans went to a special table near the front, where the teachers were sitting.

The metal covers were telekinetically raised and moved out of the way. My mouth watered at the sight of roasted vegetables, meat, creamy pasta, and mashed potatoes. If there was one thing that connected all of the students, it was their hunger. Using our powers drained our bodies and a nutritious diet combined with plenty of sleep were essential.

Everything was delicious. For a moment, we were able to forget about the looming competition and the ignore the fiery glances that some of the west campus students would shoot in Ryland's direction every now and then.

After dinner, there was a crackle and a woman's voice echoed over the intercom system "The opening ceremony will begin at eighteen-hundred hours. Please stay with your campus group and make your way to the auditorium." Her voice was robotic and cold, she sounded like AI.

I looked around; no one could hide their nervousness. A little further down the table I saw Katie with her small group of goth friends. She met my eyes and her lips arched in a small smile.

"This is going to be great," Phylicia said. Her pink acrylic fingernails clicked on the metal table.

Luke nodded. "The opening ceremony is always my favorite part."

Ryland and I exchanged glances. The stress weighing down on him was visible. He wasn't sitting tall and defiant like usual. "Hey," I said and held his hand under the table. "Don't let them get to you."

Ryland's expression hardened. "I wont. I'll show those dicks what real power looks like. They'll regret the shit they said to me."

His voice was icy enough to send a chill down my spine.

The bell rang to mark the end of dinner. One by one the tables of students were guided out of the mess hall and towards the auditorium. All of the teachers from the west campus wore crisp black and gray uniforms. They stood tall and proud, looking like soldiers at attention. The Dean commanded enormous respect and it showed.

When it was our turn, we followed the other students towards the auditorium.

"I'll be really glad once this stuffy formality is over," Phylicia said as we walked.

"It's not going to be like this the whole time?" I asked.

"Oh my god, no!" Phylicia laughed. "At least, I hope. Last year, after the opening ceremonies we were able to explore however we wanted." She added.

"Yeah, but that wasn't at the west campus," Ryland said as he looked over his shoulder. "Dean Kennedy is something else."

I really didn't want to walk around like I was in a military parade all week, so I hoped he was wrong.

The auditorium was as grand as I expected it to be. We filed in and took our seats quietly. The initial energy that radiated from the groups of students was gone. Even the east and south campuses' students looked serious. Not as serious as the west campus, but enough to put me edge.

I sat between Ryland and Phylicia, gently touching Ryland's knee to reassure him.

He looked over and forced a smile. "Don't worry about me," He whispered.

Truth was, I wasn't worried about him. He had shown that he could take care of himself just fine. It was me that I was scared for. I had a fraction of the training that other students had. I couldn't compare to them, no matter what my teachers said.

As if sensing my anxiety, Ryland leaned over to me. "Hey, don't be nervous. Once the rules get explained, I think you'll realize that you really do belong here. Trust me. You're more powerful than you think."

I smiled. If I hadn't known better, I would have thought he was reading my mind; too bad my mind was blocked from his powers for a reason we both hadn't discovered.

The lights dimmed and the whispering stopped. All four deans took the stage, along with a professor from each campus. Ms. Blackwell stood beside the Major looking as proud and flawless as ever. There were some men in suits at the back of the stage. I didn't know who they were, but they looked important. The government crest was projected onto the curtains behind them. The same pair of eagles that was on the flag at the north campus.

"Good evening students. I hope dinner was too your liking." Dean Kennedy spoke loudly, addressing each campus in turn. "I am very proud to be hosting the twenty-third annual National Competition. The National Competition is a time for the newest generation of psychics to showcase their talents for future employers in both the public and private sector. The list of employers is heavily classified, so the only way to know who is watching is to be hired." His lips twitched with a smile. "As is tradition, the students who are coming to the end of the training will be assessed first. Everyone else, this is your chance to hone your skills and meet your peers."

The speech dragged on. I sank back in the surprisingly comfortable chair and stifled a yawn.

"Each talent will be divided into active or passive groups. You will be paired with those with similar talents and those who might be more challenging. You will show how you use your skills in battle, in problem-solving, and in every day tasks."

Finally, when Kennedy stopped talking, the excitement began.

Each dean called a student forward from their campus. I didn't recognize the girl who stood next to Major Griffiths. I must have seen her in the cafeteria at some point, but I didn't have any classes with her.

"How long do students normally stay here, anyways?" I asked.

Ryland glanced over. "Depends on the student and the skill. Some stay for one year and some stay for four. I don't think anyone has been here longer than that, unless their powers manifested very young."

When I enrolled, I was convinced that it would only be a year. I knew now that I'd probably need more time to hone my skills before I was considered in control and employable. The Federal Psychic Academy didn't play by the rules like a traditional school. Every single path was different, but that was probably for the best. How could each skill be shoved in a simple box anyways? It would be impossible.

"Who is that?" I asked, meaning the girl who stood by Major Griffiths. She was tall and thin, with long blond hair and a sun-kissed tan. She stood proudly on the stage as the representatives from the other campuses made their way down the aisle.

"Zoe McMahon," Phylicia said with a slight edge. "One of our resident mean girls. If you don't know her, consider yourself lucky."

Once all four students were at the center of the stage, Kennedy approached them all with a stony expression. "As the key holders for your campuses, do you swear to uphold the rules of the competition and to act with dignity and compassion?"

"Yes, sir." The four students said in unison.

"Show me your talents." The dean demanded. He held out a rubber ball like the ones I used to train with.

Zoe stepped forward. She raised her hand and focused. There was a hum in the air as her psychic powers awoke and suddenly the ball flew up into the air, hovered and then lowered itself back into the dean's hand. She stepped back and bowed her head.

The next student stepped forward. He was from the east campus, the gold stripe on his uniform glittered in the stage lights. He gave a curt nod to the dean and took the ball from his hand. A fire erupted in his hand, shooting flames high up over the stage. Then, it vanished in a curl of smoke. The ball was singed, but unharmed.

A wave of whispers rolled through the auditorium.

Phylicia took a sharp inhale beside me. Her hands were gripping her seat and the upholstery was smoking.

I nudged her. "Are you ok?"

She snapped out of her shock and pulled her hands away from the seat, crossing her arms over her chest. "Yeah," She said. "Just, never seen another pyrokinetic my age before." She added.

I was so distracted that I didn't see the talents of the other two students being displayed. All of the students were whispering. Pyrokinesis was a very rare talent. Phylicia sat beside me utterly speechless. I'd never seen her like this before.

"What, uh, what campus is that boy from?" She asked.

"East," I said.

She didn't reply. She only fanned herself with her hand. Heat pulsed around her. It was so strong I felt as if I were sitting by a bonfire.

I felt something shimmering in the back of my mind. It wriggled softly and the energy around me hummed. Things were going to get very interesting. I don't know how I knew that. I just knew.

CHAPTER THIRTEEN

I was woken by the sound of a trumpet the next morning. The ear-splitting tune was played over the intercoms in every room of the dormitories. I groaned and threw my pillow over my head.

"Come on, sunshine." Phylicia was already up. Her bed was made. She was showered, dressed, and even had her make up done.

I peeked out from under the blankets. "How do you have so much energy?"

"No reason, just looking forward to the competition." Phylicia flashed me a brilliant smile and went back to reapplying her plum colored lipstick. She hummed as she perfected her full pout.

I hid back under the blankets. "What time is it?"

"Five AM."

I groaned again. One day, when I graduated, I would find a job that let me sleep in until 10:00am. I was no morning bird, that's for sure. I felt Phylicia plunk down on my bed and poke my foot.

"Let's go, sleepy head." Phylicia said.

I sighed and threw the blankets and pillow off of me. "Ok, fine." I dragged myself out of bed and got ready as fast as my tired bones would let me. Phylicia waited for me, humming to herself and checking her make up in the mirror every ten seconds.

We arrived in the lobby at the same time as Ryland and Luke. I was surprised to see them. "I thought you two would be using the training room already," I teased.

Luke shook his head. "After yesterday, I needed sleep."

"Isn't it sad when six thirty is considered sleeping in?" I joked. The other three shrugged, it was normal for them now. "Anyways," I coughed. "Let's go get breakfast."

Ryland's hand brushed mine as we walked. "Hey, I know you're trying to keep things cheery, but the competition is serious business." He whispered. "Maybe try to dial down your tone a little. We need to keep our heads in the game, and so should you."

How could I keep my head in a game that I didn't even know the rules for? I lifted my chin slightly. "Sure, I'll keep that in mind."

We served ourselves a protein-rich breakfast from the buffet and found our tables.

No one was mixing with students from the other campuses.

"When will the schedule be announced?" I asked in between bites of omelet.

Phylicia shrugged, rolling her spoon around her in tofu scramble. She seemed on edge, always looking towards the door any time someone walked in.

I ignored her nervous glances the first few times, but my curiosity got the best of me. "Phylicia, what are you doing? You seem on edge."

Phylicia forced a smile. "No, it's nothing."

I knew what it was by the tone of her voice and how her face darkened in embarrassment. "It's the pyro guy, isn't it?" I leaned forward and whispered.

Phylicia feigned shock. "What? No. No way?" She dropped her voice. "Is it that obvious?"

"No, but I had a feeling," I said, shrugging it off to make her feel better. "If it matters, I think you should go for it."

Phylicia looked away. "I dunno, I don't have much luck in the love department."

"You never know until you try," I said, inwardly groaning at how cliché that sounded. Who was I to give out advice about love? I had two guys falling for me and so far I couldn't even decide. Ryland was the bad boy I craved, while Luke was the reliable guy I could depend on. Then there was Daniel. I had nearly forgotten about him in all the excitement. I nearly forgot how we almost kissed. Almost.

"Ok, girls, ready to get our schedules?" Luke said. He had polished off three plates of breakfast.

Suddenly my stomach didn't feel so great. I exhaled to calm my nerves and forced a smile. "Absolutely!" I lied. My eye met Ryland's, and he gave me a discrete smile. He was probably as nervous as I was, but he'd never let it show.

The competition schedule was posted on screens outside the cafeteria. Students were lined up to find their names under all sorts of different headings. The noise and crammed bodies was overwhelming. I hovered near the back until some of the students had moved out of the way.

Ryland put a reassuring hand on the small of my back.

"So, uh," I looked up at him. "How does this work, anyways?"

"Find your name, it's alphabetical. Your schedule is posted there. There's three main divisions of skill testing: combat, problem solving, and everyday tasks." Ryland explained. He was more helpful than anyone else had been so far. He craned his neck to get a better look. This competition could decide the fate of the graduating class. I just tried to stay out of the way as usual.

The crowd thinned and Luke and Ryland pushed their way through. Phylicia snorted something under her breath before shouldering past the other students. They had strength where I had none, but I could use my small stature to my advantage. I slipped in between two south campus students who had tried to block me.

The screens were huge enough to read from almost any angle. They scrolled upwards slowly; I waited for the "H" section.

Hall ... Hampton... Herb ... Hernandez. There! Bianca Hernandez (North) - Round 1 Telekinetic Task - Telekinetic Sparring - Round 2 Problem Solving ...

My first event was in the everyday task section and I breathed a sigh of relief. Something easy should get me warmed up. I noted the time and locations of each of my first round tasks before slipping back out of the crowd. The air was noticeably cooler when I wasn't surrounded by bodies.

Luke popped up a minute later, having literally teleported ten feet in order to get out of the crowd. He had a huge smile plastered on his face. "So, what's first for you?"

"Telekinetic task, nine o'clock." I said. "You?"

"Sparring is first for me,"Luke beamed. I had never seen him so excited before. "We spar with students in the same talent group and then it gets harder." He explained. "The sparring matches are popular, so come by if you want to watch. My first match is at ten."

I made a mental note. "Sure thing," I said.

Phylicia pushed herself out of the crowd next. She was literally shaking with excitement. "Oh my god," She said. "Oh my god."

I looked at her. "What?"

"I'm starting with sparring tomorrow afternoon. Which means I might go head-to-head with the pyro from east campus!" She squealed and then regained her composure. She forced herself to keep her voice low. "I'm freaking out."

"Yeah, I see that!" I laughed. "Maybe it's meant to be." I teased.

Phylicia rolled her eyes. "Don't get my hopes up."

"Sounds like I'll be watching a lot of sparring," I said. "I'm starting with the tasks division and I'm not complaining." Maybe it wasn't as flashy as sparring, but that suited me just fine. I needed to start this slowly. I had barely sparred at my home campus without cause trouble, I'd be terrified to spar in front of a crowd.

When Ryland came back through the crowd, he didn't look thrilled.

"What's wrong?" I asked.

"Everyday task for me. I was hoping to spar," He said flatly. "I have to wait until tomorrow."

"They're probably afraid to let you spar," Luke said, but he was only half-joking.

"Let them be afraid, it won't change anything. I'm going to win." Ryland spat. He looked to me. "What about you?"

"Everyday task at nine," I said.

"Uh, it's almost nine." My three friends said in unison.

"What?" I glanced at the clock reading 8:51 and gasped. "Holy shit, I gotta go!"

Luke grabbed my hand. "I'll get us there. What room?"

"Main building, 240" I rattled off from memory, which was nothing sort of a miracle.

"Good luck!" Phylicia said.

I glanced at Ryland just as Luke teleported us out.

A moment later we were in the main building. Thank goodness we had a tour the evening before or else I'd have no idea where to go. My vision blurred as I caught my breath. The combination of teleportation and nerves had my stomach in a knot. I grabbed the wall to keep me upright.

"You ok?" Luke put his hands on my shoulders.

I nodded, swallowing hard and not trusting myself to speak. "Give me a second." I croaked after a few more deep breaths.

The hallway was nearly empty. It was a long corridor with a few doors and bright lights. It looked like the inside of any other school and far less impressive than the buildings that had been renovated before the National Competition.

I straightened up and looked at the door before me. 240. "Ok, so I guess I just walk in?" I said meekly.

"Yep. Sorry, but I won't be able to wait for you." Luke said.

"I know. I'll try to make it to your match." I promised.

Luke reached out to touch my hand and a bolt of energy shot through us. Maybe our connection wasn't as strong as the one between Ryland and I, but I hadn't exactly been fair to him either. That kiss in the classroom. That night in the dorms. Luke was amazing, but I was so blinded by my lust for Ryland to notice. I felt the heat rising in my cheeks and pulled my hand away. "Thanks for teleporting me." I fumbled over my words.

Luke pushed his hands into his pockets. "No problem. I should get back. Good luck."

"You too." I said, watching him disappear.

I braced myself and focused on the task at hand, gently knocking on the door. I knocked again. No answer. I took a deep breath and twisted the handle open, finding a simple white room.

It was much smaller than a normal classroom, lined with mirrors at the back of the room. A shiver down my spine told me I was not alone and a glance towards the camera in the corner confirmed my suspicions. This was strange. A single desk and chair sat at the center of the room. My footsteps echoed as I walked towards the desk and found a paper taped to the top.

Dear contestant, in order to respect the anonymity of the judges and the employers, the room will be empty and monitored remotely. Please perform the task assigned to you.

"Complete the task?" I whispered. "What the heck is the task?" I glanced around. The room was almost completely bare, except for a large bin on the floor. I crouched down to inspect it, realizing that it was full of colored shapes, a mix of all sorts of colors. "What the hell?" I whispered.

Instructions were taped to the top.

Please arrange all shapes according to color by only using telekinesis. Any physical contact with the bin or the shapes will be an automatic fail.

"Sorting shapes? What kind of everyday task is this?" I shook my head and stepped back.

An alarm beeped and the digital clock on the wall burst to life, the timer ticking down from twenty minutes.

My heart jumped into my throat. Twenty minutes? But there were thousands. I took a deep breath and focused on the bin. There were so many tiny pieces, how was I supposed to latch onto just one? There had to be some trick to this.

I flexed out with my powers, sifting through the plastic shapes, watching them swirl around the bin as if they were caught in an invisible whirlpool. I narrowed my focus, trying to pin point one single shape, but it seemed impossible. How could I feel just one if I put my hand in there? It was the same feeling, but in my mind.

I shook my arms and took a step back, pacing and glancing at the clock. These pieces were the size of a coin, way smaller than anything I had ever practiced with before. What was the trick?

Fifteen minutes remained.

"Shit," I breathed and rolled my head back and forth. Ok, now was not the time to freak out. Fifteen minutes was plenty of time. I closed my eyes and pushed my energy towards the huge bin of shapes. I worked through the pieces, letting them swirl and move against the force. I found myself in a relaxed state very quickly. The soothing sound of plastic pieces moving against each other like waves filled my ears. How could I latch on to one piece at a time and sort them all? It was an impossible task.

No. It was an impossible task if I didn't think outside the box. I extended my power and flipped the box upside down, sending the plastic shapes all over the floor. Now that they weren't so close together it should be easier to get a feel for them.

My fingertips tingled as I let the feeling pass through my mind. It was then that I noticed the slight differences. I closed my eyes. One shape felt round, one felt smooth, one was sharper, one was rough. I sorted through them all, seven feelings in total, that soon became distinct in my mind as if I were seeing them.

That's it! I focused on the round ones, sending them up into the air and opened my eyes. To my surprise, it wasn't the circles that were hovering at my eye level. It was the yellow pieces. Yellow felt round? If I hadn't done it myself, I'd say I was on drugs. I lifted the yellow shapes higher and gathered them together in a floating ball.

I smiled to myself. I'd show those judges something they hadn't seen before. Now that I had it figured out, it was time to show off.

I reached my energy out to the smooth ones next, the blues. I gathered them into a ball next to the yellows. Next was the sharps. Red. Rough was green. Squishy was purple. Bumpy was orange. Last was the cold-feeling pieces. The white.

In less than a minute, I had all seven colors floating above me in nearly perfect spheres. I was amazed at myself, but didn't let it show. I breathed in and out slowly to calm my nerves. With a slow twist of my wrists I let the colorful balls lower to the ground and arrange themselves in the order of the rainbow, with white at the end. The plastic pieces settled on the ground in neat piles with barely a sound. I stepped back and put my hands on my hips.

The buzzer rang again, and the clock stopped. I had finished the task with six minutes to spare. I let my powers recede, feeling the familiar tingle at the base of my skull.

There was a crackle and a robotic AI voice spoke over the intercom. "Thank you, contestant. You have successfully finished the first task. You are dismissed."

I glanced around the room. I figured the anonymous judges were watching be behind the mirrors or through the camera, or both. I backed away from the piles and didn't take a breath until I had closed the door behind me.

Relief flooded me like a wave. My legs suddenly felt like jello and I sank to the ground with an emotional gasp. I did it. I had done the task flawlessly with time to spare. I could barely believe it myself.

"Bianca, are you ok?"

I looked up to see Ryland leaning against the wall. I smiled and jumped to my feet. "I'm better than ok. I did it!" I squealed and pulled him into a hug. I kissed his cheek before I fully realized what was happening. "Wait. How did you find me?"

"I found your schedule on the screen. I wasn't about to let Luke whisk you away and not follow up." Ryland said. He held me tightly. "I was worried about you. I know these challenges can get intense, and it's not like you've had as much practice as most of us."

"It was amazing," I said. "A simple task, really." I added with a humble shrug.

"Good," Ryland said with a smile.

A group of west campus students walked by, shooting wary glances at Ryland. They were silent until they thought we were out of earshot. "So, anyway, are you guys going to watch the sparring?" One asked his friend.

That reminded me. Luke's sparring match was today and starting soon. "Do you want to come watch the sparring with me?" I asked.

Ryland's cold expression warmed slightly at the thought. "Absolutely! Come on, I can't wait to show you the training arena."

∞

For what seemed to be the hundredth time since yesterday, I was completely blown away by the west campus facilities. The training arena made our facility look abysmal. The arena was modern with a sharp utilitarian architectural design. It looked more like a stadium than a gym. There was enough tiered seating for a few hundred guests. The main floor was divided into six equally sized sparring areas divided by tall plexiglass walls. Scratches and dents from previous matches dotted the gleaming plastic.

A huge screen on the wall showed the matches as they were scheduled. Luke was up a few minutes. He was matched with a student from west campus. The arena was buzzing with energy; many seats were filled with west campus students, eager to cheer on their own.

"How does this school afford all this?" I asked, gesturing around.

Ryland chuckled. "Private donors. Silicon valley money," He said. "They get way more funding than we do back in Detroit." He looked around, his expression unreadable.

This used to be his home turf. I had no idea how he was feeling. I gently touched his knee. "I'm glad you came to Detroit. I wouldn't have met you otherwise," I said. Just as I leaned in to kiss him, an announcer spoke over the crowd.

"Ladies and gentlemen, please focus your attention on square 6."

I tore my eyes away from the pair of students sparring with telekinesis and saw Luke standing in the middle of a square. He was paired against a student with blond hair and glasses. He was gangly and thin, but I knew better than to judge someone with psychic powers based on their physical appearance.

Ryland sucked in a breath and nearly choked on it.

"What's wrong?" I asked.

"That's Kevin Spooner," He said. "The kid that got me expelled."

CHAPTER FOURTEEN

Luke and Kevin stood facing each other at the center of the square. The area was completely empty. Nothing for them to use to fight except themselves. They were motionless, staring each other down like hungry wolves and waiting for the buzzer to signal the start of the match.

"Hand to hand combat?" I squeaked. "What if someone gets hurt?"

Ryland leaned forward in his seat. "Sparring matches only last nine minutes. That isn't enough time for anyone to do serious damage," He said. "It's more of a test of your skills than actually trying to hurt the other person. For those of us who want a job in the military or law enforcement, fighting is part of the game."

I shivered. I had no interest in anything like that. I'd be quite happy to return to a normal mundane life once I graduated. But I had a feeling that I wouldn't be so lucky not after everything that had happened to me these past months.

The buzzer rang out, and the crowd cheered. I couldn't see any panel of judges, only countless cameras capturing every angle of every match. The anonymity of whoever these judges were creeping me out.

Luke was the first to make a move. He lunged and vanished just as he got close enough to touch his opponent. Kevin whirled around, his fists at the ready, expecting Luke to reappear behind him. I had seen Luke spar, and this was one of his tricks. Luke teleported above Kevin and slammed him down to the ground.

Kevin lay motionless for a second on the cushioned floor before bolting to his feet and teleporting to the corner of their square. He was bleeding from his nose.

"Yes!" Ryland said, clenching his fists. He edged forward on his seat. "Kevin was always such a whelp," He said.

I wasn't so sure. The screens showed closeups of the pair as they fought, and I could see an intensity in Kevin's face that I hoped Luke didn't miss. He was angry and I could sense that this would be a tougher fight than Ryland thought it would be.

The crowd grew louder. The majority of them were west campus students, cheering for Kevin. East and south students were concentrated on the other squares and cheering for their own.

My eyes flicked to the telekinetic students. Their match had finished. One girl was nursing a split lip.

Ryland gasped, and I looked back to Luke's square. Kevin had Luke in a choke hold, pulling at his jaw. Luke managed to kick him off and stumbled back. Kevin wiped blood from his nose and shouted as he lunged again.

Luke nearly lost his footing as he vanished and reappeared at the opposite corner. Once he caught his breath, he teleported behind Kevin, grabbing him and throwing him to the ground.

"I can't believe it," Ryland said under his breath. "Luke is better than this. How is Kevin of all people giving him a run for his money? Pathetic."

Luke wasn't weak. He was more dedicated to training than anyone else in the academy. This struggle wasn't because of Luke's weakness, it was because of Kevin's strength.

When the buzzer rang, both boys were battered and bloody from the fight. A teacher came in to literally separate them. She used her telekinesis to seize them and pull them apart. Both were breathing hard and chomping at the bit to get one last punch in.

The announcer spoke over the crowd. "In the match of Luke Herrington North Campus versus Kevin Spooner West Campus. The judges have called a draw!"

Boos and hisses erupted from the west campus students.

Ryland shook his head. "Unbelievable."

I sank down in my seat, relieved that the match was over, and covered my face with my hand. My heart was pounding in my chest. Never before had I seen a sparring match where blood was spilled. I wasn't ready for this. No way. Mental tasks were one thing, but I didn't want to hurt anyone.

"Come on," I said to Ryland. "Let's go make sure he's ok."

"I was actually thinking I could take you back to my dorm room for a quickie before I have my task this afternoon." He grinned.

I glared. "You know I'd love that, but this really isn't the time." I worked my way through the aisles and down the steps to the main floor of the area. A glance over my shoulder confirmed that Ryland was following, albeit slow and under duress.

Luke was standing away from the crowd of west campus students and patting his face dry with a towel. His shirt was soaked with sweat and blood.

"Luke!" I shouted and ran the last few steps. "Luke, are you ok?"

Luke looked up and his eyes met mine. "Do I look ok?" He snapped.

I was taken aback. I stopped in my tracks, barely noticing when Ryland bumped into me.

"Sorry. I watched your match. It was great. I wanted to make sure you were alright." My voice faded away.

"I'm fine." Luke threw his bloody towel in a bin beside the water fountain.

"Hey, just because you lost to Kevin doesn't give you the right to talk to her like that!" Ryland stepped between us.

Luke's eyes blazed. "I didn't lose." He fired back. "It was a draw."

"Yeah, a draw against a loser like him." Ryland snapped.

Luke clenched his teeth and shook his head. "I don't have time for this."

I recoiled under Luke's poisonous glare. I had never seen him so mad before. I stepped aside as he brushed past us and into the change rooms.

The west coast students were watching us. I looked their way, and they quickly avoided my glance.

Ryland glared at them. "What are you looking at?"

The thin blond boy who had fought against Luke pushed through the crowd. He smirked at us. "Well if it isn't Ryland Williams. I'm surprised they let you back on the grounds after what you did last winter." He sneered. His face was washed and free of blood, but his nose was bruised. "How dare you show your face around here after you nearly killed me!"

Ryland braced himself. "I didn't try to kill you!" He fired back. "Your weak ass just couldn't teleport properly. It's your fault you almost ended up in limbo."

"I know you were playing with my thoughts. Telepathic people like you can't be trusted once you get in our heads."

Ryland growled low in his throat. "I wasn't doing anything. I've told my story a thousand times. You were weak. That's it." He turned on his heel.

"Am I really?" Kevin called after him. "Pretty sure I kicked your friend's ass back there."

Ryland whirled around. "You got lucky."

"Do you think I'd be lucky again? Want to try me? A lot has changed since I saw you last. It might be interesting."

"You're not worth my time." Ryland spat.

"Oh so you're scared then? I bet you couldn't face me in the arena." Kevin continued to dig into him with his words. "Afraid to lose in front of your girlfriend?"

"I don't lose." Ryland hissed. "I can take you any time, any place."

"Hmph, alright. Then meet me here after hours and we'll see who's better." Kevin said. He grinned and put his hands on his hips. The other west coast students watched and waited like a pack of hungry coyotes.

Ryland hesitated. He stared back at them, his jaw flexing as he weighed his options.

"Ryland, you can't, if you get caught," I tried.

Ryland held up his hand to silence me. "Fine by me," He said. "I'll meet you here tomorrow night. No crowds, no cameras, just us."

Kevin chuckled. "Oh, I look forward to it." He took a step back and vanished into the crowd of students.

I had a bad feeling about this. "Ryland, you shouldn't have let him get to you." I put my hand on his shoulder, but he shrugged me away.

"Don't worry about it, this is between me and him." His voice was dark. "I'll finish this once and for all. Kevin Spooner will regret the day he met me and fucked up my life. I guarantee it."

8

I spent the rest of the day on my own. Both boys were too caught up in their mental battles to want company, and truth be told, I couldn't stand being near either of them when they were like that.

I went to the mess hall for lunch and sat alone. I didn't want to bother with anyone right now. I needed to focus on what was next. I ate my rice and beans slowly, wondering who I was going to be paired up with for sparring. Up until recently, I hadn't even thrown a punch before. Although I knew that I had what it took to kick ass, it didn't mean I wanted to do it on a regular basis. I still had nightmares of the night that I fought those Rogues. Knowing they were still out there only made it worse.

I pushed the rice around with my fork, suddenly losing my appetite as the stress took over. My next event was scheduled for tomorrow morning. Maybe I could drop out of the competition? It wasn't like anyone would be interested in hiring me, anyway. I couldn't control my powers as well as my peers. Sure, I was strong, but so was a wildfire. Strong but uncontrolled and dangerous. That's how others saw me. Which seemed to be all that mattered in this place.

My eyes wandered around the mess hall. Groups of students huddled together while they ate and talked. No campuses were intermingling. I looked down at my blue bracelet that marked me as a student of the north campus. While I had originally hoped that I could meet some cool people, the competitive attitude made me want to hide.

A blond girl with a blue bracelet walked by. Zoe. The one from the opening ceremony who had been totally upstaged by the pyro boy. She walked fast, with purpose and sat down with some other girls from our campus. I recognized one from my class with Ms. Blackwell, but I had forgotten her name.

I tapped my fingers on the cold metal table. Maybe it wouldn't hurt to talk to them? Wait, no. She was telekinetic, which meant we were rivals here.

One of them must have caught me staring. They whirled around and glared at me.

I tried to look away, but it was too late.

"Do you have a problem, girl?" Zoe snapped from a few seats over.

"Nope." I sighed, picking up my tray and standing up. "Just leaving."

"Ha, good. Learn your place. If you end up facing me, you're going to wish you were dead." Zoe shouted after me.

I emptied my uneaten food in the garbage and walked out of the mess hall as quickly as I could.

CHAPTER FIFTEEN

Apparently, the word got out that we had a pyro match. Something that hadn't happened in years. It was the last match of the day and the other sections had been emptied just in case. Pyrokinetic power was as dangerous as it was rare. Everyone had turned out to watch the match on the second day of the competition.

"Ladies and gentlemen, please focus your attention on square 3." The announcer's voice was loud enough to shake my bones. I gripped the edge of my seat. Everyone had turned up for this sparring match. Everyone except Ryland. I couldn't see him anywhere. Luke sat on one side of me, while Katie and her group of goth friends were a few rows over.

I had never seen Phylicia in action before. I was half excited and half terrified. Her braids were bundled into a giant bun. She wore a full body catsuit of black flame-resistant material. It shimmered under the arena lights. If I had to pick a word to describe her, it would be: badass.

The person opposing her was also dressed in flame resistant clothes. He was standing with his arms crossed over his chest. He had tanned skin and dark brown hair. His body was lean, strong, and he was incredibly handsome.

"We have a very rare match up for you today. May I present Phylicia Booker of north campus and Julian Alviar of east campus." The announcer continued.

Someone from behind me was talking to their friend. "I don't think he should be allowed to compete. You know he's an exchange student from Europe? There's no way this is fair!"

I resisted the urge to look over my shoulder at the girl who was speaking. Exchange student? That meant there were other campuses all over the world for psychics? The thought was nearly unfathomable. I shrugged it off and glanced at Luke.

He looked exhausted from his match. A dark bruise blossomed on his cheek. Luke sensed my gaze and glanced at me. He forced a tight-lipped smile but said nothing. Everyone was on edge. Even friendly and dependable Luke. Katie didn't seem much better off. She was always quiet, but there was an unusual energy about her today. The entire mood was unsettling, to say the least.

The announcer spoke again. "Here we go!"

Geez, this was like a effing boxing match! Everyone else was excited, but I was terrified. I fixed my eyes on Phylicia. She looked cool and calm. She stood with her hands on her hips. Her expression was unreadable from this distance.

A buzzer rang out, and the fight began. Phylicia made the first move. She raised her palms to the ceiling and flames burst from her hands.

Julian matched her ferocity, balling his fists and summon flames that swirled around his hands.

Pyrokinetics was one of the lesser understood physic phenomena. Those with the power to manipulate the environment to produce a flame at their will seemed something out of a fantasy novel and not real life.

There was a brief moment of stillness before they lunged at each other.

Nine minutes. That's all they had to last for. Nine minutes and it would be over. If someone didn't get killed first. I chewed my bottom lip, watching them shoot fire back and forth. They were both fast and agile, a perfect match.

Phylicia dodged the flames and flipped off the plexiglass wall. I could see her taunting him with a huge grin on her face. She was moving with confidence and grace.

Julian didn't get worked up by her attitude. He remained in control of his fire.

The heat reached the audience now. The arena's exhaust fans kicked on to clear the smoke and reduce the heat. A bead of sweat rolled down my neck.

Neither of them landed a single hit. They both kept their distance. Fire was not a weapon for close contact sparring. I began to wonder who would run out of energy first. Phylicia's stamina was impressive, but her flame was waning.

Julian saw his advantage and sent a fireball towards her, catching her side as she dodged. Her fireproof bodysuit was undamaged.

I fought the urge to look away. The time limit was quickly approaching. Just a little longer and it'd be over. My nerves couldn't take it. I gripped the edge of my seat until my knuckles turned white.

Luke was tense, leaning forward to get a better look and holding his breath whenever one of them struck.

The noise of the crowd had fallen away now. The only thing I could focus on was the match. It felt as if the world was in the background. I had tunnel vision. The only thing I cared about was Phylicia coming out of this unscathed.

The buzzer rang out to signal the end.

Phylicia and Julian both attempted one last shot before backing away from each other. They were covered in sweat and smeared with soot from the arena floor, which had barely endured the ordeal. The heat warped the plexiglass walls.

The crowd cheered and shouted for more.

"The judges have determined that this match is a draw." The announcer said over the speakers.

More cheers and boos bubbled up from the crowd. I leaned back in my seat and let out a long breath. It was over. That was possibly the most intense nine minutes of my life and I was grateful that Phylicia was on my side. I'd hate to fight a pyro after seeing that.

∞

I went straight back to my room after the match. The boys (Ryland and Luke) were both nowhere to be found and I didn't have time for their mind games. They were obviously too focused on the competition to even bother with me. Especially Ryland. I hadn't seen him since the argument with Kevin. I wanted to tell him not to go through with the fight, but he'd never listen to me. There was no doubt it my mind that no matter what I said, Ryland was going to show up to the arena after hours and destroy Kevin, as well as possibly get kicked out again.

I sighed into my pillow and rolled over. The blank ceiling stared back at me, cold and indifferent. The room was nice enough, but the homesickness was getting harder to ignore.

The door opened with a bang and Phylicia walked in. She smelled like smoke and ash.

"Phylicia!" I bolted up in my bed. "Are you ok?"

"Fine," She said with a shrug. "Just in need on a shower." She sniffed her clothes, which no doubt smelled like smoke too.

The crazy thing was, I believed her. Phylicia was never once to mix words or try to save face. She had never told me anything but the truth. She seemed pumped, energized even, after her fight. "You were incredible." I said.

"Thanks," She grinned. "I haven't had a fight that good my entire life." She was positively beaming.

"So, is he taking you out on a date after that?" I asked, leaning forward so I wouldn't miss a word of the story.

Phylicia shrugged and smiled. "I don't know. He didn't ask. But, wow he is so sexy up close. Like, I swear his looks distracted me more than his fire." She giggled like a little girl.

"If he didn't ask, then you should," I said.

Phylicia's eyes widened. "Oh my god, no. I couldn't do that." Her voice trailed off as she considered the option. She shook her head. "Maybe. We'll see." She opened her suitcase. "So, what are you wearing tonight?"

"What do you mean?" I asked.

"Tonight is the gala." Phylicia's mouth fell open. "Wait, you mean, no one told you about the formal event?"

My face burned red. "No. It seems that people forget to tell me a lot of things lately." I shrugged. "It's fine," I lied. "I just won't go. I can't. All I have is training clothes."

"No way! The gala is the best part of the competition. It's the only time we have to be normal before the rivalries take over and people are too beat up to look good in pictures." She laughed at my horrified expression. "I'm joking. Kinda."

"I have nothing to wear," I said.

Phylicia flashed me a crafty smile. Her dark brown eyes glittered. "Honey, you just leave that to me."

CHAPTER SIXTEEN

I don't know how she did it, but Phylicia actually pulled it off.

In her suitcase, among the dozens of potential outfits, she had a stretchy convertible maxi dress. She draped the amethyst-colored fabric around my waist and tied over my shoulders like a halter top before wrapping the excess around my waist. The X shaped fabric across my torso was the only thing keeping my boobs from making a surprise appearance.

"You small-chested girls can always get away without a bra," She sighed wistfully. "There, what do you think?"

"Phylicia, it's amazing, thank you." I looked myself up and down in the mirror. It was simple but elegant and fit like a dream. No one would have guessed that it wasn't my dress.

"Girl power," She winked. "We gotta stick together, right?" Phylicia had chosen a fitted cocktail dress in a brilliant sapphire blue with pumps to match.

I slipped my feet into my ballerina flats, thankful that the dress was long enough to hide them. In less than an hour, she had transformed me from an exhausted paranoid student to an elegant woman. I was literally speechless.

'Well, let's get going. I'm sure the west campus is itching to show off more of their fancy facilities." Phylicia rolled her eyes. "Let's make the most of it."

∞

Phylicia hit the nail on the head.

The ball was held in a literal ballroom that had been built onto the main building, especially for this event. It was modern and white, like everything else, with countless tables for people to sit and a dance floor to mingle. A purple glow emitted from the low lights and candles flickered on the tables encased in ultra-modern silver centerpieces.

"Wow." My mouth fell open what I saw it all.

As I took it all in other students walked around me, entering in pairs or groups. Everyone wore suits and dresses, and they radiated sophistication. The group of psychics who had been thrown into fighting rings only hours before cleaned up good.

"Let's go get a table," Phylicia grabbed me by the elbow and guided me to a table. "So, are your moody man friends going to be joining us?" She asked once we sat.

I opened my mouth, then hesitated. "I don't know." I suddenly felt deflated and weak.

"Hm. I see," She said slowly. "Well, don't let it ruin your night. Seriously. The competition does weird things to people's heads." She paused. "This one might just be extra special, considering the history of all those involved."

I looked up from the centerpiece and nodded. "You're right. I'll just give them space." It killed me to say it, but it was probably the best thing I could do. It wouldn't be easy, not when I knew that Ryland was worked up into a frenzy and Luke wasn't even speaking to me.

More students were filling the room now. The music was still low enough that we could speak at a normal volume, but the chatter was growing louder. The students had still segregated themselves according to campus: blue bands on the north, white bands on the east, red bands on the south, and black bands on the west. It was a small marker that weighed heavy with meaning.

"Why aren't people trying to get to know each other?" I wondered out loud.

Phylicia gaped in surprise. "Can you blame them? The competition comes first, everything else is second." She shook her head. "It's just how things are. I know I'm graduating this year, which means I have to pour my soul into this and land a good gig after school."

That was the other thing I had a problem with. We were busting our asses for people we couldn't even see. Why? The whole event just didn't sit well with me. I had a strange feeling about it; it was probably nothing, but it still bothered me.

I had enough to worry about. Like the people back in Detroit that were going missing. Like the Rogues who were still after me and would most definitely kidnap my family if they found out their identities. I should have pulled out of the competition when I had the chance, but I didn't want to be the only one that looked weak. Almost everyone from all campuses attended, whether they were fit to graduate or not. I wouldn't be the one that stood out, I had done that enough. I'd get through this, one way or another.

"Speaking of boys," I said, happy to change the subject to get myself out of my increasingly depressing thoughts. "Do you think your little fire beau will show up?"

That got Phylicia's attention. She sat up straighter and took a quick glance around the ballroom. "I don't know. Maybe? Why? Do you think he will?"

I smiled to myself. I had never seen her this flustered. "I don't know, but if he does, promise me you'll make a move on him."

Phylicia fanned herself with her hand. "Oh gosh, I don't know. You know he spoke to me before our match? He said he wasn't going to go easy on me. He has the most amazing English accent." She gushed, a dreamy look in her eyes.

"What did you say?" I asked.

"I told him to give me his worst. I'm not afraid of a good fight." Phylicia grinned and let a spiral of flame flicker along her knuckles.

"The match was incredible." I couldn't recall a moment where she didn't have me on the edge of my seat. "You fought beautifully."

"And so did he," Phylicia sighed. "Girl, if I didn't know me better, I'd say it was love at first sight."

As if on cue, Julian walked in, flanked by two other guys from the east campus. He was dressed in a black suit with a red tie. The east campus white bracelet wasn't even enough to clash with his designer watch.

I nudged Phylicia. "Speak of the devil."

"And he shall appear." Her voice went quiet, and she looked away quickly. "Oh my god. Why is he so perfect?"

"Go for it." I nudged her again.

Phylicia tensed and shook her head. "No. I couldn't." She protested as Julian disappeared into the crowd of students on the dance floor.

"This might be your chance," I said in a sing-song voice and raised my eyebrows. "He could be your one true love." I fluttered my eyelashes.

She rolled her eyes and shoved my shoulder playfully. "Oh, screw off." She laughed. "You're the one with men falling at your feet, not me."

Is that how people saw it? I hoped not. I was trying to keep a low profile with this whole dating thing. Guess I wasn't doing as good of a job as I thought. I gnawed at my bottom lip. Anxiety swirled around in my stomach again. I just had to keep things under control until we got back.

Time went by in a blur. After dinner, we danced for hours and I finally let go of my worries. Every time I remembered that Ryland and Luke weren't there, I pushed the thought away and focused on all the delicious man-candy from the other campuses. It wasn't against the rules to look, after all.

The clock was approaching midnight when I nudged Phylicia again. Julian was standing by the refreshment tables alone. "Now's your chance!" I squealed in her ear.

Phylicia didn't need any extra encouragement. She was off in a flash, weaving through the dancing bodies towards Julian.

I watched for a moment. There was definitely a spark between the two of them, no pun intended. Once I was sure that Phylicia was deep in conversation, I struggled out of the crowd to get some air. Being less than average height had its disadvantages when surrounded by people.

I stepped out into the hall, letting the cool air wash over me. Every square foot of this place was air-conditioned to the extreme, not that I was complaining. I took the moment to catch my breath, my body still buzzing from the energy in the ballroom.

I was plunged into my thoughts as the silence settled down around me. Luke. Ryland. It would have been so much better if they had come with me. Competition or not, it was good to let loose and have some fun. Goodness knows I hadn't been letting myself relax much lately, unless you counted my "physical therapy" sessions with Ryland.

Footsteps echoed down the hall. Whoever it was, they were running fast.

I looked up and didn't believe my eyes. Luke? "Luke!" I shouted.

Luke stopped mid-step. He wore a white dress shirt and black trousers, as if he had planned on going to the gala and then changed his mind halfway through buttoning up his shirt. "Bianca!" He sounded out of breath.

I had never seen Luke out of breath before. Come to think of it, I hadn't ever seen him run like that before either. Teleporters didn't need to run when they could just pop in and out of wherever they pleased.

"I've been looking for Ryland everywhere. Have you seen him?"

"Ryland?" I repeated. "No, I figured he was in the dorms sulking." There was more edge to my tone than I intended. "Why? What's wrong?"

Luke slammed his fist against the wall in frustration. "Damn! I knew he'd run off and do something stupid."

My eyes widened in realization. "You mean. Kevin Spooner?" I asked. "Kevin challenged him yesterday after you left. Do you really think he'd go along with it. He's on thin ice as it is."

Luke and I both knew that Ryland wouldn't back down from a challenge.

"Of course, he would. He blames that kid for everything." Luke growled and wiped the sweat from his brow. "Where were they supposed to meet?"

"The arena." I had barely finished uttering the word when Luke grabbed my hand and transported us there in a blink.

The air rushed around me as we materialized at the ground level. I stumbled, but caught my footing.

The arena was dark and quiet. It was almost unrecognizable in this state. I shivered and hugged my arms against myself. Goosebumps spread down my arms. "I don't like this, Luke." I whispered.

Luke was alert and ready for a fight. His muscles were coiled tight and his eyes flicked back and forth.

"There's no one here." I whispered.

Luke shushed me, focusing on the silence. "No, someone was here. They teleported not long ago."

"How can you tell?"

"Teleporting takes a lot of psychic energy. More than almost any other talent. We're bending physics for fucksakes! So, when someone does, it leaves behind an energy signature. Like a pulse." Luke explained. He held his breath, reaching out with his hands and trying to pinpoint where the energy signature was strongest.

I closed my eyes, trying to get a grasp of whatever he was feeling, but failed. Everything was cold and eerie. There was no psychic energy besides our own.

"There." Luke said, pointing at the center of the 6th square where he and Kevin had fought. "It's there." He led the way through the darkness.

I was barely able to make out the shadowy walls around us. "We should probably get a teacher," I said, clinging to his hand and doing my best to ignore my sweaty palms.

"No way, want to get him expelled again?" Luke said. "We need to do this ourselves."

"You really do care about him, don't you?" I mused.

"No," Luke said, irked. "I just want to preserve the name of our campus is all." He didn't sound convinced.

"You know, you two can be rivals and friends. It's not mutually exclusive." I continued.

"Hold that thought." Luke said and touched the floor. "Here! This is where they teleported out of the arena."

I stared at the spot as if I were expecting it to glow or give me any sort of sign that Luke wasn't screwing with me. I focused where his hand was and finally felt the smallest pulse. The psychic signature. "Whoa," I whispered.

Luke stood up. "You should stay here."

What? No way!" I protested. "You're not going to drag me out here and then tell me to stay put. If you're going to save Ryland, then I'm going with you."

Luke opened his mouth and then closed it. "Fine." He knew better than to argue with me at this point.

I smiled and grabbed his hand. "Well, what are we waiting for? Let's go get him." I closed my eyes and cleared my mind.

Luke knelt down and touched the energy signature.

I opened my eyes. I had no idea where we were. It was dark. We were outside in the middle of the desert. I shivered and hugged myself. "Holy shit, I forgot how cold deserts were at night."

Luke laughed. "Didn't you learn anything from the Magic School Bus?"

I rolled my eyes. "You're so funny."

A flash of light blinded me. I looked away, blinking and muttering. "What the heck was that?"

Shouts echoed in the distance and the light flashed further away.

Luke grabbed me and pushed me into the sound. Held a finger to his lips, and we listened.

One of the voices sounded like Ryland. "Bring us back, Kevin."

"No way!" The other voice shouted. It was Kevin, no doubt. "Let's see how much you like being left out in the middle of nowhere!"

"Fuck off, I never meant for you to get stuck in limbo. Let it go, asshole!" Ryland shouted back.

Luke and I inched forward through the rocks and sand, catching a glimpse of the fighting pair. They were both battered and bloody, dressed in clothes that belonged in the gala, not in the middle of the desert.

"What are we going to do, Luke?" I whispered.

Luke watched them exchanging blows. "I guess Kevin's plan was to kick his ass and dump him here."

"Where's here?"

"The Mojave Desert, I'd guess."

I shivered. "That's just cruel. What the hell is wrong with this guy?"

"I will have my revenge, Ryland!" Kevin screamed. "You know what I went through after you screwed me up? They wouldn't let me teleport for months. No one trusted me with my powers, and it was all because of you."

"I still wouldn't trust you with your powers." Ryland spat. His lip had split, and he was sporting a black eye. His white shirt was stained with dirt and blood.

Kevin didn't look any better. He wiped the blood from his nose. He shook his head and laughed hysterically.

"We need to stop them," I whispered.

Luke shook his head. "Let them duke it out," He said. "If we interfere now, we'll only make it worse. As soon as Kevin teleports back, we'll grab Ryland."

"You're being serious?" I hissed. "No way. I don't want him getting hurt."

"Ryland won't forgive us if we stop him."

"I don't care. I'm not going to just lay here in the sand and watch them kick the shit out of each other."

"Then what do you propose?" Luke asked.

I flexed my fingers and grabbed hold of a large rock with my psychic connection. Ever since the test yesterday morning, I was ultra aware of the feeling of different objects when I held them. It was different than a physical touch, something that corresponded to the material itself, the most basic molecular make up. I focused my energy on Kevin and psychically threw the rock at him.

The fist-sized rock hit him in the side of the head. Kevin stumbled and hit the ground hard.

"What the!" Ryland exclaimed. He looked in our direction and his eyes grew wide.

I scrambled to my feet, nearly tripping on the hem of my dress. "Ryland, are you ok?"

Ryland stood motionless with his hands dangling at his sides. He looked at me and then at Kevin. "How the hell did you do that? How are you here?"

I closed the distance between us and hugged him tight. "Luke and I were worried, so we followed you."

Ryland didn't return the embrace. He stood their cold and stiff. "I see."

Luke jogged over and nudged Kevin's foot. "He's unconscious, hopefully that rock didn't do any damage."

I released Ryland and looked him in the eye. "Are you ok?" I asked again.

Ryland sighed and avoided my eyes. "Yeah, I'll be fine." The blood on his face was drying.

"What happened?" Luke asked.

"I agreed to spar with him in the arena. He grabbed me and teleported us here." Ryland gestured around vaguely. "I had it handled; you didn't need to save me."

Luke shot me a "I told you so" look.

"Ryland, he was going to abandon you here. We don't even know where here is!" I shouted. That was it. I had enough of his loner bad-boy attitude. He needed to start realizing that he couldn't do everything on his own. "What if he would have left? What would you have done then? In the middle of the desert with no water and no way to find civilization!"

"I would have been fine." Ryland shrugged me off and walked away, running his fingers through his blond hair.

I watched him pacing.

Luke put a hand on my shoulder. "Just leave him be," He said. "He's embarrassed and frustrated, that's all. He'll come around."

The tension left my body. I fought off tears as I spoke. "I just wanted to help."

"I know," Luke said and wrapped his arm around my shoulders. "Unfortunately, there are a lot of people in this world that don't want help." He paused. "Let me take you back and I'll come back for Ryland."

I blinked in surprise. "You're going to leave him here?"

"Just for a second," Luke promised. "I'll pop you back in the dorms and come right back. I think maybe he just needs to be alone."

I let out a shuddering sigh and wiped my eyes. I stared at the back of Ryland's head. He was tense, not speaking and not acknowledging us at all. "I guess that's fine," I said and grabbed Luke's hand. "Please take me back."

Luke nodded and in a flash, we were back in my dorm room.

Phylicia had not returned, things must have been going well with her pyro crush.

I collapsed backwards onto my bed and let out a frustrated growl. Sand fell out of the creases in my dress.

"Let it go," Luke said. "Ryland will come around."

"Why does he have such a problem with people caring about him?"

"I don't know," Luke said with a shrug. "Try to get some sleep. I'll do my best to reason with him. Don't waste your energy, you'll need it for your sparring match tomorrow."

My heart skipped a beat. I completely forgot about that. "Great." I sighed and rubbed my eyes, probably smearing my makeup, but I didn't care.

Luke gave me one last look and then teleported out.

I let the silence settle around me. I was so done with this stupid competition. Nothing was turning out like it was supposed to. My chest ached with disappointment and exhaustion. I just wanted to go home.

CHAPTER SEVENTEEN

"Ladies and gentlemen, please focus your attention on square five!"

The announcer's voice rattled my body. Everything was so loud in this plexiglass box. I felt like a fish in an aquarium. My heart was going a mile a minute. My hands were sweating. My mouth was dry. I stared across the square at the other telekinetic girl.

Wendy Tanaka from west campus. The crowd wasn't cheering for me; they were cheering for her.

I didn't let it get to me. I'd just get through this match as best as I could and survive to fight another day. That was my new plan. I braced myself when the buzzer rang, dug my heels into the mat and raised my fists.

I had one thing to my advantage: everyone underestimated me. No one, not even the students of my own campus, knew what I had been through with the Rogues. No one knew that I had real fighting experience outside of the ring. No one knew that I had to literally fight for my life only a month ago. They thought I was weak, and that's where they were wrong.

Wendy smirked at me, tossing her black hair over her shoulder. "Ready?" She taunted as she levitated off the ground.

Her powers were telekinesis and levitation. Great. Nothing I couldn't handle.

"You asked for it." I said through gritted teeth, letting my energy flow down my spine and to my hands. In a blink, I had her in my grasp, squeezing and throwing her to the ground.

Wendy screamed as I let go. Her eyes blazed with embarrassment. "Fine, you get that one. But I'm done playing nice." She reached out, attempting to get a hold of me, but I fought back against her energy.

"Listen, Wendy," I grunted. "I don't even want to be here, so let's make this quick." I threw myself back, breaking out of her psychic hold.

The announcer was saying something. The crowd was screaming. I ignored it all to focus on the task in front of me. "Come on Wendy, get up."

Wendy stumbled to her feet and began to levitate higher. She screamed at me, sending her powers towards me in a random and rapid pattern.

I dodged them, moving closer and closer to her until she was backed into a corner. "That's a cool trick," I said, pointing to her feet. "Too bad I can do it too." I focused my energy on my own body and easily lifted myself off the ground. Sure, it wasn't true levitation, but it freaked her out just the same.

Wendy stammered, her psychic hold was weak.

I grabbed her with the invisible force and shoved her against the plexiglass wall. She fought desperately, but her energy was not strong enough to overpower me. It was almost too easy. I kept her pinned until the buzzer rang. I let go, and she fell to the floor, gasping for air.

"The judges have determined a clear win for Bianca Hernandez, north campus!" The announcer shouted. "Totally unprecedented! A new student!" He jabbered on, but I shut it out.

I walked out of the arena in a sort of daze. That was too easy. When did fighting come so naturally to me? Me! The girl who never even threw a punch in high school. The girl who cried instead of yelled. I was beginning to think that there was more behind my powers than I had been told. There was a reason those Rogues were so obsessed with me, and I was certain it had something to do with this.

"You did great today."

I looked up. I hadn't expected Ryland to forgive me for saving his life so quickly. "Thanks," I said and went back to my lunch.

Ryland sat down beside me. "Sorry for how I acted yesterday," He said. "I was just embarrassed that I let myself get tricked by that asshole. If you and Luke hadn't came, I'm sure I'd be wandering the desert right now."

I let out a dry laugh. "Do you know how many times we've had this conversation, Ryland?"

Ryland raised his eyebrows. 'What do you mean?"

"The usual. I do something. You're rude to me. The next day you apologize. Then we're all good for little while until I do something else to piss you off again." I shook my head. "It's exhausting."

Ryland was speechless. Finally, he spoke. "Bianca, you know how much I care about you. I'm just not good at this sort of stuff."

My heart ached for him. "Then stop pushing me away and getting mad at everything, Ryland." I said, looking him in the eye. "I like you too, but I can't deal with this hot and cold."

Ryland nodded somberly. He leaned in and kissed my cheek. "I know. I'll try to do better."

I let the topic drop for now. "So, what happened last night anyway?"

The blond boy groaned and drummed his fingers on the metal table. "That jerk cornered me in the arena and teleported me to the middle of the desert. And well, you know the rest," He said. "He was still unconscious when Luke came back. I said we should leave him but Luke wouldn't. We dropped him back on the campus grounds and that was it."

"Aren't you worried he's going to report you? You'll get expelled. Again."

"No. He won't say a word because he's afraid of getting himself in hot water, too," Ryland answered and took a sip of coffee. "I've decided to let this grudge go, but if he ever comes after me again, it'll be the last time." His blue eyes were hard and dark, burning with anger.

I nodded and looked around the mess hall. Since the gala, students from other campuses seemed to have opened up to one another. I caught a glimpse of Phylicia. She was sitting at the east campus tables and holding hands with Julian. She was glowing with happiness. Fire talent aside, they really did make a cute couple.

Ryland nudged me. "Hey, earth to Bianca."

I snapped out of my daze. "Whoops, sorry."

"Luke's final match is today. Are you going to go watch?" Ryland asked.

"What? Already?" I was surprised. "This week is going by so fast."

"Not fast enough," Ryland muttered as a group of students from the west campus walked by. "I'm tired of all the glares. I just want to get back to Detroit."

"Really?" I asked. "But this is your home."

Ryland chuckled and shook his head. "Honestly, Bianca, I'm starting to think my home is wherever you are."

His words warmed me. I looked down at my empty plate and smiled. "I know what you mean. I' so glad that we're here together. I don't know what I'd do without the support of my friends."

"And more than friends," Ryland leaned in and kissed my cheek. "Have I ever told you that you're sexy as hell when you're sparring?"

I blinked in surprise. I had no idea he was in the audience during my match. "No," I said with a shy giggle. "I didn't think I looked very good at all, actually."

"You are," Ryland said earnestly. "You're a badass fighter, even if you don't think so. I'd bet you could totally win your division if you put your mind to it."

I shrugged off the compliment. "Maybe. I guess."

Ryland kissed my cheek and nibbled gently. "Maybe we should go give you some extra training, privately?"

Heat flowed through my body at the thought. "Hm, I would love unwind after that sparring match, if you have any ideas." I tipped my head innocently.

Ryland grinned, lustful fire burning in his eyes. "Come with me." He grabbed my hand and took me away to his dorm room.

CHAPTER EIGHTEEN

I entered the plexiglass room. The crowds were screaming and shouting, eager to see the next round of sparring matches. The box diagonal to me was the main focus, where two telepathic students from the south campus were at each other's throats.

I forced myself not to listen.

"Ladies and gentlemen, the next match will be in square three." The announcer said. "Bianca Hernandez from north campus and Zoe McMahon from north campus."

My stomach dropped as she entered the box. She had a smug look on her face.

"Zoe is the favorite of the telekinetic division this year," The announcer went on and I blocked him out.

"Looks like they thought you'd be able to take me," Zoe said with a grin. "What a mistake.

You're that new girl who likes to run with the boys right? What's your name again?"

"Bianca." I said through clenched teeth.

"Oh right, that's it. I forgot." Zoe laughed and flipped her hair over her shoulder.

The buzzer rang out.

"Let's just get this over with," I said and raised my hands.

"I thought you'd never ask." Zoe replied. She clenched her fists at her sides and grabbed me with her energy, tossing me into the air and onto the mat.

I gasped; the air knocked out of my lungs. I looked up at her from where I lay, trying to come to my senses.

"Pathetic," Zoe said. "You're out of your league, girl." With a flick of her wrist she sent me flying against the plexiglass wall.

The crowd cheered and gasped in awe.

This was no good. I was getting my ass kicked. I couldn't end the competition like this. I struggled to my feet and held up my hand to block her telekinetic grasp. She was strong. Her energy surged forward and pushed against my own. It was all I could do to hold her off.

"I'm not playing, Bianca. Can you survive these nine minutes?" Zoe taunted.

I let the tingle at the base of my neck awake and pushed out with my psychic energy. I grabbed for her, but she dodged. We stopped at opposite corners of the box. There was no need for close contact fighting when we could use our minds.

Zoe attacked again with a hair-raising shout.

My feet slid against the mat as I pushed her energy away. I had to think fast. Going against her energy was not going to cut it. I had to be creative. There had to be another way. I paused to think, my fingertips twitching at my sides.

Zoe stopped to catch her breath. She pushed her long hair out of her face and locked eyes with me. "Giving up?"

"Never." I said. Then I had an idea. If there was no way to stop her from attacking me, I'd just have to trap her somehow so she couldn't get to me. I glanced around. There was nothing but plexiglass walls and a cushioned floor for me to use.

Two minutes. I had to survive the next two minutes and hopefully impress the judges enough to make up for the beginning of the match. I used my energy to grasp and pull on the plexiglass wall behind her.

It felt different from the metal I had bent before. It didn't bend to my will as easily. The wall creaked and groaned, pulling against the bolts that held it in place.

Zoe jabbed out at me with her psychic connection, but I managed to dodge. I pulled harder on the wall and a bolt sprung loose. The announcer was jabbering something, and the crowd was growing louder. I couldn't focus on them, I had to focus on winning the match.

Zoe heard the second bolt pop and she realized what I was doing. She rushed forward, attempting to claw at my face.

I used a swift right hook and my fist collided into her eye socket. She fell backwards and the plexiglass bent around her, trapping her against the wall. I pushed the plexiglass against her to make sure she couldn't move.

"You fricken bitch!" Zoe shouted. She struggled to squeeze out of the trap and failed.

The buzzer rang again. The match was over.

I let out a sigh and leaned against the wall opposite her. The plexiglass groaned as I pulled it back up enough to let her escape.

Zoe fell to the ground panting. Staff came running in to check on her.

Someone grabbed me and pulled me out of the box. It was Ms. Blackwell. Her expression was cold and unreadable. She dragged me through the crowds. "That was unbelievable, Miss Bianca," She said. "But, I do believe we agreed for you not to attract attention to yourself."

I couldn't tell if she was angry or proud. Maybe a mix of both?

I struggled to keep up with her as she walked, still gripping my arm tightly.

A staff member of the west campus stopped us at the door. "Stop right there," He said. "Deliberate destruction of academy property is an instant disqualification."

My mouth fell open. "What?"

Ms. Blackwell held up a hand to silence me. "Can we discuss this privately?"

The man hesitated and then nodded.

Ms. Blackwell let go of my arm and turned to me. "Go back to the dorm, I'll deal with this."

I nodded dumbly, watching her walk away. Once she was out of sight, I pushed through the crowd and ran as fast as I could to the dorm.

I threw open the door and ran head first into another student. We both went flying backwards. I groaned. "Sorry," I muttered as I stood up.

"Girl, what the hell is going on?" It was Phylicia. Seeming completely unphased by our collision, she helped me stand back up.

I rubbed my forehead where it had collided with her chin. "The competition," I said.

"Oh was your round today? Oh my god, I'm so sorry I missed it. I was hanging out with, you know." Her voice trailed off.

"It's ok," I said with a shake of my head. "I think I just need to lie down."

"What happened?" Phylicia asked.

"Just got out of hand. Seriously, it's fine," I said.

Phylicia looked me up and down suspiciously. "If you're sure."

"I am. Just need a nap." I tried to make my tone as convincing as possible. "I'll see you at dinner, ok?"

I climbed the stairs without looking back and felt a wave of relief wash over me as I got to our room. I tapped my bracelet against the sensor and the door slid open.

"Hey." A voice stopped me just as I was about to walk in.

I turned around to see a girl with curly platinum blond hair. She was from north campus. I didn't know her name but I knew she hung around with Zoe. Great. "What's up." I tried to keep my voice steady.

"You really screwed up that fight, you know," She said. She was shorter than me. Petite and cute but with a deadly look in her eye and a scowl that ruined her otherwise pretty features. "How could you embarrass our start student like that? Zoe didn't do anything to you."

"I was just sparring!" I protested.

The girl looked me in the eye. "Don't worry, I'll make you pay for what you did." She grinned.

My head started to throb and my psychic energy pulsed down my spine. She was trying to get into my head. I wanted to look away but my body wouldn't listen.

My hands raised on their own and the dorm room shut. She was controlling my body. I couldn't blink or speak.

"I could make you do anything I want," The girl teased in her sickeningly sweet voice. Her curly hair bounced as she walked around me. "I could even make you jump out the window."

I struggled to speak. To say no. To shout for help. Nothing worked. She had complete control over my body.

Just to prove her point she tilted her head to the side and I mirrored her. I felt like a stranger in my own body as she made me turn around in a circle. "No one messes with my friends," She said.

What could I do? I couldn't even blink. My eyes were stinging and tears rolled down my cheeks. I was terrified. How could I get her to let go of my body?

"Hey, what's going on?" Ryland came up behind us. He was panting as if he had run all the way from the main building to find me.

"Nothing." The blond said and cut off our connection. "We were just chatting."

I moaned and fell to the ground.

Ryland dropped to his knees and pulled me close. "Bianca!" He glared at the girl. "What did you do, Clary?"

"Nothing." She giggled and skipped away.

"Clary? Do I know her?" I mumbled.

"She's in my telepathy classes." Ryland scooped me up in his arms and opened the door with my bracelet. He laid me down in bed and wiped the tears from my cheeks. "What happened?" He asked again.

"It was terrible." The fear flooded from my body and more tears flowed from my eyes. He dabbed my face with a tissue. "She had control of my body, Ryland. There was nothing I could do to stop her."

Ryland held me close. "She's a twisted one," He said. "I'm sorry."

"If you hadn't come, I don't know what she would have made me do. She was mad because of my fight with Zoe. I didn't mean to cause trouble. I was just doing by best." I tried to catch my breath as I sobbed.

"It's ok," Ryland said as he rubbed my back. "I won't let that happen again. I can teach you how to defend your mind from people like her. It's not easy, but I'm sure with practice you can do it."

I nodded and rested my head against his shoulder. "They're going to disqualify me for destroying the square." I was quiet for a moment and then chuckled. "God, what a week. I can't wait to go home."

Ryland and I sat in content silence for a while, lost in our own thoughts.

"My last match is this afternoon. Will you still come cheer for me?' He asked after the silence became too heavy.

"Of course," I said. "You know, I think being disqualified is kind of a relief. I wasn't ready for this."

"Yes you were, you did great. It's the academy that has stupid rules." Ryland kissed my forehead. "You're an amazing psychic and I know that you will totally rock at whatever you decide to do with your life. Don't let this place bring you down. Don't worry about the politics. I should have learned that lesson a long time ago." He looked at me and smiled. "You're something special, Bianca. I love you."

∞

I chose the best seat for Ryland's final sparring match. Ryland was facing off against a guy from the south campus. He stared him down like a hungry wolf. He was tense and still, a perfect fighter waiting for the buzzer to ring.

I gnawed on my fingernails. I hated to watch him fight as much as I loved it. He was amazing when he was in the zone. The way he fought was almost beautiful in a way that anyone looking from the outside wouldn't understand.

Ryland hadn't lost a single match. He was a flawless fighting machine. I was in awe of his talents. I bet the west campus was regretting losing him now.

The buzzer rang. Ryland made the first move, lunging forward and lashing out with both fists.

"I wonder what his opponent's talent is." Luke said.

I looked over. "Wouldn't it be telepathy?" I asked.

"Not in the final match. They get matched randomly." He glanced over at me with a teasing grin. "You'd know that if you hadn't been disqualified."

"Hey!" I poked his shoulder. "Too soon."

"I'm kidding," Luke said with a chuckle. "Your match was fricken awesome. Totally worth getting disqualified, in my humble opinion. The way you bent the plexiglass. Amazing." He shrugged. "Sucks that Ms Blackwell couldn't get them to make an exception. Bet they would if you were from west campus."

"Honestly, I'm fine with that," I said. "Fighting is so not my thing."

"But you're great at it." Luke said with a smile.

I blushed. A gasp from the crowd got my attention back to the match as it unfolded. The small cubes for sparring were cleared away to allow more movement for the main event. Ryland didn't use the space, he kept close to his opponent, locking eyes with him and reading his every move.

"Does that guy know Ryland can read his mind?" I whispered.

"Nope, they go in blind to the match. Neither of them have any idea, unless they've come to watch before. Even then, you never know. A lot people have more than one talent." Luke explained.

I leaned forward to get a better look. So far Ryland's opponent hadn't done anything but block punches. Whatever his talent was, either it was very weak or it was being saved for something big. Based on his status in the finals, I'd bet it was the latter. His opponent was young to be in the finals, about fifteen, which solidified my suspicions that he must be hiding a powerful talent.

Ryland's opponent lashed out with his fists, dodging the attacks as they came. He was avoiding Ryland's eyes to protect him from telepathy.

I tapped my knees. "Come on, show us your power," I whispered. The suspense was killing me. I wanted to know what Ryland was up against.

Suddenly, Ryland was thrown against the wall by an invisible force.

"Telekinesis." Luke and I whispered together and exchanged a look.

"Why did he wait so long to show it?" Luke wondered out loud. "What kind of strategy is that?"

"Whatever it is, it must be good for him to have gotten this far," I said.

"I think Ryland can take some telekinesis after everything he's been through," Luke said and glanced at me. "No offense. It'll just come down to how well the other guy can keep his mental blocks up."

The crowd hissed as Ryland landed a punch on his opponent's jaw.

"Looks like Ryland can take this," I said, but nothing was ever as easy as it seemed.

Ryland was grabbed by the psychic connection and thrown against the wall. He came down hard and didn't move.

"No!" I gasped. "Oh gosh, please get up Ryland, please get up!"

"So this kid's expertise is brute strength." Luke observed. He was strangely calm.

Ryland struggled to his feet before being knocked to the ground again. Blood was flowing from his lip. He wiped the blood away on the back of his hand and grinned, more blood flowing from between his teeth.

"Now we're getting somewhere," Luke said. "Watch this."

"Huh?" I blinked and looked closer.

Ryland had entered pure blood lust. His look was psychotic as he stood and focused his energy on his opponent. With two minutes to go, he'd really have to do something great to impress the judges. He didn't charge in headfirst like he would normally do, instead he stood calmly, his eyes focused on the prize.

Ryland's opponent suddenly went blank. His eyes glazed over and he stood as still as a statue.

"What's happening?" I gasped.

Luke grinned. "He's in the kids head. Telepaths can do a lot more than read minds, you know. He's blocking his mind and holding his body."

A shiver ran through me. So Ryland could do the same tricks that Carly could do. Controlling bodies. I didn't need another reason to be glad Ryland was on my side, but I added it to the list anyway. I swallowed hard, watching Ryland count down the last minute with his opponent completely helpless.

Ryland could have made the kid do anything, but he didn't. He kept this opponent still and his dignity intact. When the buzzer rang, he released him without showing off. He put his hands in his pockets and waited for the judges to announce the winner.

"The judges voted six to four for Ryland Williams." The announcer shouted.

Ryland went over to his opponent and helped him up. He was talking to him quietly to make sure he was alright. The kid shook his hand and smiled.

I let out the breath I was holding and sank back down in the chair. Luke was on his feet cheering and I just was happy the fight was over. I knew it was wishful thinking, but I hoped that I'd never have to watch a sparring match that stressful again.

CHAPTER NINETEEN

"Ok , now I need you to focus." Ryland stood in front of me. We faced each other in the student gym dedicated for psychic training. It was late afternoon and the room was empty.

"How is this going to work if my mind blocks you?" I asked with my hands on my hips.

"Just trust me. You can feel when I try to read your mind right?"

"Yeah, unless you've gotten better at it. It's creepy as hell."

Ryland laughed. "It feels different for everyone. What's important is to be able to know when someone is trying to access your mind. Telepathic people have a variety of talents. That girl Clary can influence the mind and body better than I can."

"Terrifying." I shuddered.

"I don't disagree. The best defense against psychics like her is to avoid eye contact and put your mental blocks up." Ryland stepped back from me until we were just out of arm's reach. "If she gets in your mind and you aren't strong enough to kick her out, the results can be, well, deadly."

I shivered as I remembered her threatening me. She could have made me kill myself. She could have made me do anything. The power she had was beyond terrifying.

Ryland locked eyes with me and concentrated.

I felt his energy trying to enter my mind. My forehead tingled and the feeling grew into a sharp pain. I closed my eyes and looked away.

"Ok, so you can feel me?" Ryland asked. "Good. Your thoughts are still shadowy and unreadable to me, but at least you can get familiar with the sensation."

I shook my head and groaned. "It's a strange feeling."

"Normally it's a lot less invasive, we just have a weird bond." Ryland explained. He'd never been able to read my mind since we met. "Ok, get ready I'm going to do it again."

"How do I stop it?" I asked.

"You know the feeling when you get a weird thought and you try to push it away or think of something else? That's the trick. Put up a wall by filling your mind with other thoughts. Push back." Ryland explained.

The pain returned as he pushed into my mind again. I clenched my teeth and stared back, bringing up any thought I could think of to keep him out. I gathered my psychic energy and instead of letting it flow to my hands, brought it up to my head.

"Visualize the block." Ryland instructed, not letting up.

As he pushed harder, I felt the power over my body waning. I would not let anyone control my body like that again. Summoning all my strength, I imagined my powers creating a shield around my mind, forcing his energy away from me. I created a barrier out of my energy and thoughts.

Ryland broke off the connection and took a deep breath. "Better," He said.

I wiped sweat from my face. "It's intense." I stretched to relieve the tension in my body.

"Let's go again. I'm going to transmit a message. When my thoughts go silent, it'll mean that you've successfully blocked me out."

I nodded and braced myself for the uncomfortable twitch that I felt whenever he tried to enter my mind. It reminded me of the first time we met, when he saved me from the Rogue and spoke to me in my head. Who would have thought we would have come so far?

"Focus, Bianca!"

I flinched and focused my attention away from those memories. Now was not the time. I let my power flow to my mind, forcing up the shields again.

"Can you hear me?" Ryland's voice flowed into my head. It was slightly distorted and quiet.

I forced the shields up harder, visualizing them thickening and protecting my thoughts.

Ryland's voice grew quieter. "Good. Now force me out. Don't let anyone into your mind, Bianca."

I closed my eyes and took a deep breath. My spine tingled as my power worked its way up my body and lashed out with all the force I could muster. There was a brief moment of tension before my power surged and the connection snapped. I felt the psychic shields fall into place and opened my eyes.

"Yes!" Ryland cheered. He jumped and ran to my side. "Perfect, that's what I'm talking about. Geez, you learned in ten minutes what Luke hasn't learned all year. Great job."

I beamed. "Really?"

"Yeah!" Ryland pulled me close and kissed me hard.

Reality melted away and I lost myself in his kiss. I loved his taste, his smell, his touch. Everything with him was more perfect than I could have ever hoped for. "Thank you, Ryland," I said after finally breaking away from the kiss. "Seriously, I don't know what I'd do without you."

Ryland's eyes softened. "You'd be ok. You're so powerful in your own right. I see it every time I look at you. You might had had a rough beginning, but I know without a doubt that

you're one of the best this academy has seen."
He paused. "The way you pushed back against
my telepathy was impressive."

"Well, let's just say I don't want to find out
what training would be like without your help."
I said.

"Hey, I'm not going anywhere. Promise."
Ryland kissed my forehead gently. He looked
down at me with a devilish grin. "Now why
don't you say we get some fun in before
dinner?"

∞

The competition was officially over. The
mess hall was decorated in a way that should
have looked out of place in such an industrial
setting, but somehow didn't. I walked in with
Ryland by my side. The room was buzzing with
energy and everyone was talking and laughing.
It felt good. It was a far cry from the serious
first meal we shared.

I caught a glance of Phylicia's vibrant braids
and found seats for Ryland and I. "Why aren't
you sitting with your beau?" I asked.

Phylicia looked up. "We need to sit with our
campus team," She said with a fake pout. "Don't
worry, I'll make up for it later."

"So it's going good, then?" I asked.

Phylicia giggled and looked away shyly. It
was unbelievable that one boy could make
someone as tough as her blush.

Ryland ignored our giggling and poured a
glass of ice water from the pitcher. Luke joined

us a moment later and Ryland shot him an exasperated look.

"Girls will be girls," Luke chuckled.

Ryland rubbed my knee under the table. His touch made me burn with need. We hadn't had the chance to get much further than second base before the buzzer sounded to call us to dinner. I squirmed when his hand explored up my inner thigh.

Ryland grinned at me when I slapped his hand away.

"Ladies and gentlemen," The dean stood at the podium. His dark blue suit was trimmed with gold thread that glittered in the lights. He waited for everyone to quiet down before continuing. "Good evening and thank you for your attention. It has been a wonderful week and I thank all the campuses for their efforts."

The other deans watched him from the head table and clapped politely.

"It was my honor to oversee the competition to the help of my fellow faculty members and our esteemed judges." Dean Kennedy went on.

The judges that were still anonymous. No one knew who had watched them spar or solve problems. And we wouldn't find out unless we got a job offer. It didn't matter for me though, thanks to my disqualification.

I sighed and rested my elbows on the table as the Dean went on and on. He was the kind of person who just liked to hear himself talk. Pretty much the exact opposite of our dean,

Major Griffiths, who acted as if he had never left the military.

Dean Kennedy waved his hands and our meals appeared before our eyes. "Now, let us eat. The winners will be announced shortly."

"Winners?" I repeated, looking around at my friends.

"Yeah, every competition has to have a winning team," Phylicia said. "The judges analyze our individual performance, our sportsmanship, etcetera." She took a spoonful of mashed potatoes and mixed it with her vegetables.

"Oh, I hope my disqualification didn't hurt our chances." I cringed.

Ryland touched my shoulder and I perked back up. "Doubt it. Besides, it's almost always the home team that wins. They have home advantage after all."

I watched the west campus students across the room. They were practically dripping confidence, like they had it in the bag.

Just as dessert was being served the dean stood at the podium again. "Before we dig in, I have a few announcements to make." He said. "I want to begin by saying that this years' judges were very impressed with all of you. I truly believe that it is the efforts of our community that are paving the way for psychics to reach new heights of success in both the public and private sector." He adjusted his cue cards. "Secondly, I would like to announce the winning team of this year's Annual Competition."

The anticipation swelled at the west campus' table.

Ryland looked down, poking at his dessert with his fork.

I couldn't even imagine how he felt right now. He was waiting for his old campus to win, watching them celebrate before their names were even called. He used to be one of them and now they all looked at him with fear or scorn. They had wiped his name from their records and treated him like a stranger because of one single screw up. It hurt me to see the defeat on his face. He tried to hide it, but I could tell he was angry.

"Tonight, I am very proud to announce the winning campus of the competition." The dean paused for effect, holding an envelope high. How classy. "Please join me in congratulating," He opened the paper and his brow furrowed. "Please join me in congratulating the team of," He forced out the next two words. "North campus."

The mess hall erupted in cheers. Every table jumped to their feet except the team from west campus. They sat dumbfounded and silent, staring at Dean Kennedy who looked like he shared in their collective shock.

"Oh my god, we did it!" Phylicia shrieked.

Ryland turned and hugged me tight. "We did it! Wait. What? How the hell did we?" He shook his head. "Whatever, it doesn't matter. We did it!"

"The winning team proved their capabilities in problem solving, everyday tasks, sparring, and showed good sportsmanship throughout the week. The judges agreed that they deserve the title of champions this year." The dean's voice was drowned out by the cheers.

Phylicia hugged me from behind, nearly crushing me. "We did it!"

I stood in a daze while our table screamed and hugged, all of us looking equally surprised we won but taking it in stride.

The west campus students were glaring at us silently. A few girls were crying. A bunch of people abandoned their dessert and stalked out of the mess hall without looking back.

Major Griffiths took his place at the podium and waited patiently for the cheering to stop. "Wow, how unexpected!" He said. "On behalf of the north campus, I would like to thank our judges for their time and the students and staff of the west campus for being such gracious hosts."

Luke snorted a laugh quietly and glanced at Ryland.

"As is the tradition, I will announce the host of next year's competition." Major Griffiths checked his paper. "East campus will host the competition next summer." He handed the microphone to Dean Brier.

I went back to my dessert as she spoke. I hated all these formalities and strawberry cheesecake was way more interesting. I tapped my foot in order to keep the rest of my body still. The surrounding energy grew more intense as the minutes ticked by. This many excited psychics in one place was enough to give me a headache.

People stayed at their tables until well after dinner ended. The east and south campus students came to congratulate us but the west campus students all left.

Julian came to sit by Phylicia, they glowed with happiness as they sat and talked. I sipped coffee and listened to the conversations around me, just happy to be taking it all in.

"And you, girl with the plexiglass!" An east campus student leaned over the table to speak to me. "That was amazing!" He exclaimed. "Like holy shit you deserved to win because of that."

I heard Zoe make a disgusted noise a few tables away.

"Oh, no, I got disqualified." I said. "I shouldn't have done that," I added modestly. "It wasn't fair."

"Real life isn't fair," Julian arched his neck to see over Phylicia's head. "Seriously, you were great. That sort of stuff would have gotten you bonus points across the pond," He said. "Europe's psychic academies are way tougher, trust me."

"That explains why you're so good." Phylicia said to him, twirling a braid around her finger.

I let them go back to flirting, happy to deflect the attention away from me.

Ms. Blackwell and Major Griffiths approached our table and the conversation died down. "I would like to extend my personal congratulations to you all," Major Griffiths said. "You all performed exceptionally well and impressed your peers and the judges." He smiled, glancing around the rows of tables. "We will return to Detroit tonight, so please say your goodbyes and meet in the dormitory lobby at nineteen-hundred hours."

"Yes sir," We said as one.

"Don't be late, we have a large group to teleport." Ms. Blackwell caught my eye, gave me a small smile and then left with the other faculty members.

"Finally, we're going back to our campus." Ryland sighed and wrapped his arm around me.

"You mean home?" I echoed.

Ryland shrugged. "You could call it that. But, like I said, home is wherever you are."

∞

It felt good to be back. The north campus was familiar. It was cool and dark, thanks to the three-hour time difference we hopped in a millisecond. The sky was clear enough to see the lights of the Detroit skyline in the distance.

I took a deep breath, not minding the tangy metallic taste that hung in the air thanks to the countless abandoned factories that surrounded us.

"Feels good to be back." Ryland said, as if agreeing to my unspoken words.

I looked to him and let my fingers entwine with his. "It really does." I leaned my head against his shoulder.

More students appeared in the teleportation area. We were ushered out and told to return to our dorms. I doubted anyone would get much sleep tonight. We would celebrate our unprecedented victory on the west coast's turf. It felt good, justified even. We might have left the campus as rivals, but we returned bonded and energized by our collective school pride.

Ryland took my hand and we walked back to the dorms together.

I should have been relieved to be back, but something in the air told me that much more dangerous trials were waiting for me at the north campus.

CHAPTER TWENTY

"Miss Hernandez, due to your remarkable talent shown at the National Competition, we had several employers ask for your information." Ms. Blackwell said.

She had asked me to meet her in her office after class, not wanting to share the news in front of everyone else. I didn't need any more reasons for people to hate me, it seemed.

"But I didn't win," I said. "I got disqualified!"

Ms. Blackwell waved her hand as if to dismiss the thought. "Not everything is about winning," She said. "Besides, it wasn't just your sparring that peeked their interest." She leaned back in her chair and knitted her fingers together, taking a moment to look at me in silence. "You have remarkable talent for someone who just became aware of their powers. With the proper training, there is no doubt you are going to be great."

I blushed. "Thank you." That was truly a compliment coming from as powerful a psychic as her.

"However, you are not finished your schooling and employers understand that." Ms. Blackwell continued. "All students need to be enrolled for at least a year until they are permitted to join the workforce. We need to ensure that you not only know how to use your powers, but how to control them as well."

I knew that was coming. "A year? I think I'll be needing more time than that, honestly."

"Hm," Ms. Blackwell paused. "It has been two months since you joined us and I've seen progress in you that I've never seen before. Don't compare yourself to others, you may be ready to graduate sooner than you think."

"So, what about the employers?" I asked.

"They will remain anonymous for now, but considering this, I've spoken with the Major to get you cleared for field work."

I nearly jumped out of my seat. "Field work? Like outside of the campus?" I shrieked, not believing my ears. I had begun to think I'd never be able to leave the school grounds.

"Yes, with an escort, of course." She added.

I beamed. "Thank you so much!"

Ms. Blackwell smiled and nodded her head. "Of course. Bianca, you remind me of myself," She said. "I remember feeling suffocated by the restrictions of training, especially after I had shown myself worthy of something more. What you went through last month, I'd never wish on a student, but you not only survived, you won."

"Because of your training. You inspired me," I said. Although Turner had played an instrumental role in strengthening my skills, it made me sick to credit that traitor with anything.

"The power was inside you the whole time," Ms. Blackwell said and stood. "Well, I should let you get to dinner."

I nodded. The last training session had left me starving.

"Oh, and one more thing," She said as I turned to leave. "I've lifted the security on you and relieved Ryland and Luke of their protection duties. It has become quite obvious to me that you are capable of taking care of yourself."

∞

No more escorts to and from class? It was a dream come true. I had become used to the boys' presence, and while it brought Ryland and I closer, I felt as if a stake was wedged between Luke and I. I could not deny my strong feelings for Ryland, but Luke was my friend and didn't deserve to be cast aside like I had done.

Ryland met me outside the cafeteria. "There you are," He said. "I've been looking everywhere for you."

I blinked with surprise. "Oh, Ms. Blackwell hadn't told you?" I asked.

"Told me what?"

"Uh, guess not." His question answered my question. "She called me to her office today. She said I don't need babysitting anymore," I said.

Ryland looked mildly disappointed but didn't let it show in his voice. "That's good. So they think you're strong enough to defend yourself from any Rogues that might try to come after you?"

I shrugged. "I guess so. That competition was what I needed to finally have my skills taken seriously."

"So this means I don't have to be on guard when we're hanging out," Ryland grinned.

"I guess so," I laughed. "Come on, I'm starving."

Dinner was pasta, salad and garlic bread, plus extra coffee for me. I'd never get tired of the food in this place. As I walked to my seat, I caught glances of the other students. Their expressions were different. The fear and contempt had been replaced with respect.

I sat down beside Ryland, thankful that for the first time the whispering wasn't about me.

Phylicia joined us a minute later. "Guys, have you heard the news?"

"That I graduated from needing a babysitter?" I asked. Word sure traveled fast around here.

She shook her head. "What? No." Her expression was dead serious. "Another psychic kid has gone missing."

"What?" Ryland and I said in unison.

Phylicia leaned in and lowered her voice. "Yeah, I heard two of the professors talking in the hall. Those young kids, the ones on the news, they were all being monitored for psychic talent. A bunch of them were from dual-psychic families, so they were already on the radar."

"So someone is targeting psychics who's powers haven't manifested?" Ryland asked.

Phylicia nodded.

My mouth went dry and I struggled to speak. "Rogues." I whispered. "No doubt about it."

"How do you know?" Ryland asked.

"I just do." I said. "They came after me right as my powers were revealed and they would have caught me too if I hadn't been saved." I gave Ryland's hand a squeeze under the table. "It's gotta be them."

Phylicia shook her head and rested her elbows on the table. "That's fucked up," She said. "Why are they targeting people like that?"

"To recruit new blood. They don't believe that psychics should be monitored by the government." Ryland said matter-of-factly. "We should be treated like normal citizens."

"But we're not normal citizens," I said.

Ryland shrugged. "I didn't say I agreed with it, it's just what I know." Ryland had been brought up in a family with two psychic parents. He had always known about the hidden world and the reality that psychics lived among regular people, unlike me who had been thrust into this place with barely any warning.

The thought left a bad taste in my mouth. "I can't believe we were just across the country minding our own business when something like this is happening in our own city."

"Hey," Phylicia cut in. "Don't feel bad. This isn't our war, Bianca. The feds and the police are looking into it. They have special departments for this stuff. We're just students."

I knew the government had special programs in place, but that wasn't the point. If more young psychics had gone missing, obviously something wasn't working. I had looked those Rogues in the eye and lived to tell about it, many times. They weren't giving up and no amount of FBI involvement seemed to deter them.

I pushed my plate away. My appetite was ruined now. "I'm not hungry." I stood up and left without another word.

Ryland called after me. "Hey, where are you going?"

"I just need to be alone," I said and didn't look back.

I walked straight to the training facility and was surprised to find it empty. The retractable walls were tucked away, and the training gear was all stacked neatly in it's place along the wall. It was quiet, except for the sound of fans rotating above me.

How long did I have to wait until I could make a difference? A year? Longer? Would it even matter by then? Would I just go back to my normal life or get recruited by some anonymous government agency to use my psychic skills for who knew what.

I gathered my energy, letting it flow through my body and locked onto the weights that were stacked in the corner. I lifted them one by one and let them float in a circle around me. With a flick of my wrist I could command the cast-iron to do my bidding. Up and down. Side to side. It was almost too easy. Grasping a body was harder, because they fought back against my energy.

The sound of the door opening startled me and the plates nearly fell to the mat before I stopped them midair. I whirled around to see Luke.

"Luke!" My voice echoed in the empty room.

Luke looked surprised to see me. He pulled his headphones off. "Bianca? What are you doing here? You never train after hours."

I laughed nervously. "Yeah I know. I actually just came here to think." I waved my hands and let the metal plates fall.

Luke nodded. "Same," He said. "Well, don't let me stop you." He gestured to the running track that circled the training area. "I'm just going to do some drills." He threw his headphones back on, vanished and reappeared on the running track.

I watched him run. He'd weave between the two lanes, picking up speed and then disappear. He'd teleport as he ran, sometimes jumping a few feet, other times across the facility. It was incredible to watch him move.

I tried to focus on my own exercises but got distracted every time he'd flash by me. I had been around him long enough now to notice the energy disturbance in the air whenever he teleported. It was a slight change, but just enough for me to catch.

I gave up and began stacking the metal plates back against the wall. They clanged against each other as I used my energy to pick them up one by one and add them to the pile.

Luke appeared beside me. "Leaving already?"

"Yeah," I said as the last plate slid into place. "My mind just isn't in a good space right now."

Luke stepped closer. "I heard Ryland and I were relieved of guard duty. Is that what's bothering you?"

"No. I'm happy about that." I noticed Luke stiffen and amended my statement. "I mean, I'm happy because now we can just hang out as friends. No need to be babysitting me day and night."

"Ah, I see." Luke's shoulders relaxed a fraction. "Well, then what's up?"

"In a word? Overwhelmed." I admitted and found myself leaning into him.

Luke wrapped his arms around me and hugged me tight. "Don't worry so much. I know these last few weeks have been hard on you, but you're doing great. What you really need is a vacation."

"Let me know once you master teleporting across the Atlantic and we'll go for pizza in Italy." I laughed, remembering one of our very first conversations.

Luke smiled. "I haven't forgotten."

Why was the energy between us so electric? I forced myself to take a step back, feeling my heart and mind getting caught up in his charm. Tearing away from him hurt. The way he smiled at me made me feel warm and safe. My heart belonged to Ryland, but Luke was so tempting.

"I should be going now," I said.

Luke nodded slowly. "Hey, one thing before you go. I know you and Ryland are getting serious and I just wanted to let you know there's no hard feelings."

My face burned red. "Oh, we're not. It's just casual." I stammered.

Luke chuckled and shook his head. "It's ok, Bianca. Don't spare my feelings." He rested his hands on his hips. "I know how you two look at each other. I've come to terms with it." He flashed me a brilliant smile. "I just want you to be happy. If you ever need anything, let me know."

Normally when people said that, it wasn't sincere, but with Luke I could feel the truth. I nodded and hugged him tight. "Thank you," I said. "Really. You're great."

"That's what friends do," Luke said. "Anyway, I'm glad that they've decided you can stand on your own two feet. I've known that since I met you, but you know how the older generations are. Sometimes it takes them a while to realize we're not kids anymore."

CHAPTER TWENTY ONE

We weren't kids anymore.

Those words stuck with me long after I had left the training facility. I went straight to my dorm room, reveling in the fact that I didn't have to check in with anyone before I left, and called Daniel.

Daniel answered my call in a single ring. "Bianca! I've been so worried!"

My excitement deflated. I had intended to call and tell him about the competition, but something in his tone let me know now wasn't the time. "What? What's wrong?"

"The disappearing psychics. My dad's been working double shifts all week and I hadn't heard from you. I was terrified the Rogues had gotten to you too."

I let out a sigh. "No, I'm fine. Seriously. The campus was away at an event." I couldn't believe that I forgot to tell him.

"Oh," Daniel said sheepishly. "Oh. Shit. So, I've been freaking out for nothing."

"I'm afraid so," I laughed. "But I had good news. I've been cleared to leave the campus. Turns out they finally realized I can take care of myself."

"That's awesome!" He exclaimed.

I had to hold the phone away from my ear. "Yeah," I said after Daniel had calmed down. "I was wondering if you'd like to get together tomorrow. It's Saturday, after all."

Daniel paused for a second. "Yeah, sure." I could hear the shy hesitation in his voice.

The memory of our last meeting flashed through my mind. We almost kissed. I couldn't let that happen again. Daniel was my best friend and decidedly not boyfriend material. We grew up together. It would be too weird.

"I really need a break from this crazy world," I said. "I need to feel normal for a day."

"Oh, I know. The old movie theater downtown is doing an Avengers marathon for ten bucks. Some charity thing. Do you wanna go?"

Popcorn, superheroes, and Daniel sounded like a perfect escape. "It's a date." I said before wishing I could take my words back. "I mean, I'll see you then." I forced a laugh.

Daniel's awkward laugh echoed my own feelings. "Sure," He said. "I'll talk to my dad about getting through security to come get you. How does that work anyways?"

"Don't worry about it," I said. "I'll just ask Luke for a favor. Teleporting is way better than driving." I craved normal, but some things were just too convenient to give up. Now I just had to convince Luke to take me off campus, again.

∞

Thanks to Luke's teleportation skills, I arrived early.

"You really need to chill with asking me to teleport all the time," Luke said. "I know I said I'd do you a favor when you needed it, but there's too much weird shit going on lately. If the Major found out, he'd kill me."

"Hey, I'm off the babysitting list, remember? He didn't say I had to stay on campus anymore." I countered.

"He didn't say you could leave, either." Luke said.

"Technicalities," I said with a wave of my hand.

Luke shook his head. "You're lucky I care about you," He said. "What time do you need me to pick you up?"

"Eleven," I said. "I'll meet you back here?"

Luke nodded. "Ok. Please be careful." He glanced at me as if he was going to say something but then changed his mind. "See you later." He vanished.

I walked out of the alley, hoping that no one saw our entrance. There were no screams or strange looks, so it must have gone off without a hitch.

I only had to wait a few minutes before Daniel arrived. It was impossible not to notice how handsome he looked in his classic polo and khaki shorts. His hair was lighter than I remembered it, probably because the only times I had seen him the past few months was in the middle of the night.

"Hey, hope I didn't keep you waiting," Daniel said. He hugged me tight.

"Not at all, I got here a few minutes ago." I breathed in his familiar smell of off-brand fabric softener. Here we were at a movie theater on a sunny afternoon with no worries about psychic Rogues or getting caught breaking curfew. It felt good. It felt normal.

"I'm so glad you could get out for a day," Daniel said.

"Not as much as I am!" I laughed. "Come on, let's go. I want some popcorn."

∞

We spent the next eight hours engrossed in an Avengers movie marathon. I ran out of popcorn twice.

There was no other way that I would of rather spent time with my comic-book-loving nerdy best friend. The guy who convinced me to be the Robin to his Batman for a costume contest in ninth grade. The kid who walked me home from school every day and would take the fall if we ran late because we stopped to buy candy at the 7-11.

When the marathon finally ended, Daniel shot me a look and said. "Tacos?"

"Tacos!" I agreed with a grin.

We found an authentic taco joint a few blocks away, where Daniel ordered us a family platter of carnitas with extra cilantro and fresh salsa on the side.

I lost track of time while we ate and talked. He filled me in on everything that was happening in the neighborhood, how our friends from high school were doing, even the status of the little old lady who lived around the corner and was always adopting new cats.

My heart filled with warm joy until it reached a breaking point. We talked until long after the tacos were gone, and we had been banned from anymore free soda refills.

The night was warm and calm when we finally left to make our way back to the theater. We walked in content silence, both smiling from reminiscing together.

When we stopped at the theater, I gave Daniel a tight hug. "Thank you so much," I said.

I didn't want this to end. I looked into his eyes, unable to tear myself away. The magnetic pull was stronger than last time. Spending the day with him was what I needed to remind myself of what an amazing guy he was. I was so lucky to have Daniel as my friend. I sighed.

"What's up?" Daniel asked. He held my hands gently and tipped his head, his brow creased with concern.

His big brown eyes were killing me. "I don't know," I admitted. "I just, I don't want this day to end."

Daniel smiled softly. "I know what you mean," He said with a chuckle. "I really miss the old days. Just me and you. No Rogues to worry about. No psychic powers. No curfew. No secret academies." He went on. "Things were simpler then."

I nodded slowly. "Yeah," I agreed.

There was a pause. We were frozen in time, staring at each other and not knowing what to say. The need to feel his touch was maddening.

"Do you ever wish things were different?" Daniel asked.

"Different how?"

"I mean, how it would be if you were normal."

I hesitated. Sure, this whole psychic thing hadn't been an easy road, but I had emerged from the challenges I faced so much stronger than I ever thought I would be. "Sometimes, but I don't dwell on it." I admitted. "Do you?" I turned his question back to him.

Daniel looked down. "Sometimes," He said. "I really miss you. And because of all this, I was never able to tell you how I feel."

"How you feel? You can tell me anything. You know that," I said. Daniel blushed and I realized what he was hiding. I pretended not to, but my heart started fluttering. "Daniel," I spoke when the silence became too much to bear. "I think I know what you mean. I've been thinking a lot lately."

A spark of hope lit up his eyes and it killed me.

"I swore to myself that I wouldn't let you be hurt by the psychic world anymore," I said. "I know that it ruins relationships and tears friends and family apart. I don't want to do that to you again."

Daniel looked away. "I understand."

My heart ached at the sound of his voice. I stepped towards him and hugged him, wrapping my arms around him and not letting go. "Daniel, you're my best friend. I'd never forgive myself if you were hurt because of my secret."

Daniel nodded. He hugged me back. "I know. Thank you."

"And I want you to know that I do love you. More than anyone I've ever met. You're my best friend and I know that we'll always be here for each other when things are tough." I let out a shuddering sigh as tears threatened to spill over. "But you deserve someone who you can be with every day and live a normal life. You're going to find her and when you do make sure you tell her that I say she's the luckiest girl ever."

Daniel smiled softly. "You're not going to disappear on me, are you?"

"Never." I held out my hand and wrapped my pinky finger around his like we did when we were kids. "I swear. I'll always be around, you're not going to get rid of me that easy, Daniel Dolinsky."

"Good, the feeling is mutual." Daniel chuckled and held my hands.

A pop of energy shot down my spine and Luke emerged from the alley. He stopped mid-step, not expecting to see Daniel and I so close.

"My ride is here." I sighed and let go of Daniel's hands. "This was so fun, thank you. Let's do it again soon, ok?"

Daniel nodded. "Anytime."

Luke furrowed his brow as I walked to him, no doubt noticing how red my eyes were. "You ok?" He asked.

I nodded. "Perfect."

"Ready to go?" He held out his hand.

I looked one last time at Daniel, who waved at me. "Yeah," I said and grabbed Luke's hand. "Let's go back to the academy." Where I could build up my skills enough to take down the Rogues who stalked me at night and make sure that my friends and family would be safe from harm. The psychic world was no place for them. It was my job to protect them. It was time for me to go back to where I belonged.

CHAPTER TWENTY TWO

The late summer air was cooler than I would have liked. I stood outside waiting for the professor who would be taking me out of my first field mission. Ryland and Luke got to go out on their own; I hoped that soon enough I would be trusted to do the same.

"Doubt that," A voice said behind me.

I felt the twinge in my head that meant someone had been reading my mind. I whirled around to face a middle-aged woman with chestnut brown hair streaked with auburn. She was tall and thin, with bright blue eyes that stood out like glittering gems. She had a heart-shaped face and full lips.

"Sorry to read without consent like that," She said with a smile. "I wasn't actually trying, I swear. Thoughts are very loud to me." She held out a hand. "I'm professor McTavish." She had the slightest hint of an Irish accent, she'd probably moved to America when she was a kid.

I shook her hand, putting up mental blocks to avoid her getting into my head again. "Bianca," I said. "Nice to meet you. Are you?"

"Yes, I'll be taking you out for your mission. I don't believe we've had a class before have we?"

I shook my head.

"I teach the advanced practical classes," Professor McTavish said. "You can call me Siobhan, I don't like formalities in the real world."

Her warm smile drew me in. She was beautiful and friendly and those attributes probably only enhanced her abilities to read minds. I'd bet that people naturally opened up to her.

"Are any other students joining us?" I asked.

"No, we're one-on-one," Siobhan said. "You are a very exceptional student, after all."

That was probably code for "the Major is worried about me getting someone else hurt." I shrugged off the negativity and put my hands on my hips. My new field uniform made me feel powerful: black utility pants, boots, and a t-shirt that clung to me like a second-skin. The material was thickly woven yet as light as air. I adjusted my tight ponytail.

Siobhan handed me a teleportation tracker.

"Here, put this on just in case we lose each other," She said.

I was not planning on getting separated. I slipped the tracker onto my belt loop and set my shoulders. "Alright, let's get going,"

The setting sun was casting long shadows and tinting the sky purple and pink. It was always preferred to train off campus at night, where the public was less likely to see us.

"You're eager. I like it." Professor McTavish grinned and held out her hand.

I knew the drill, grasping her hand tightly.

There was a jolt of energy and we were teleported in an instant. Now that I had teleported with a few different people, I had begun to realize the difference between the psychic signatures. Each one felt slightly different. Siobhan felt powerful and firm.

We appeared in an alley downtown. Police sirens wailed in the distance and the smell of restaurant garbage hit me full force. That stench combined with the motion sickness of teleporting was not a good mix. I leaned against a wall to calm myself.

"Lovely place, isn't it?" Siobhan laughed. "No worries, this should be an easy night for you."

"What did you have planned?" I asked, holding my hand over my nose.

Professor McTavish gestured for me to follow her. She spoke as we walked. "The psychic world is very complex, but the government keeps a tight hold on everything in order to keep the secret under wraps," She explained. "Psychics with passive powers like telepathy or premonition often end up quieter jobs than those with telekinetic or teleportation powers. Either way, most of us work in law enforcement or for the government, where our powers are best put to use."

"There must be some people who work in the private sector?" I asked.

"There are," Siobhan agreed. "But hiring those with psychic skills comes at a high premium. Very few private companies are even aware of our existence. There are obvious reasons why we need to be secretive."

I nodded, remembering how much I freaked out when I was told I was a psychic, and I had powers to prove it. I felt my mental blocks waning when she smiled at me and I increased my defenses, as Ryland had taught me. Keeping the mental blocks up was exhausting, but anything was better than the feeling of having someone in my mind.

"So, what's the objective for tonight?" I asked after a long stretch of silence with nothing but the sound of our boots on the pavement to fill the void.

"I'm sure you've heard the rumors of the disappearing psychic children," Siobhan dropped her voice and glanced at me.

I nodded. "Yes, it's all over campus now."

Siobhan rolled her eyes and laughed. "We can't keep anything from you guys, can we?

Sometimes I'm amazed that the entire world doesn't know our secret." She shrugged. "Tonight we're just going to be on the lookout for Rogues."

"Isn't that the FBI's job?" I asked.

"Yes, but we have what the FBI doesn't. Young psychics to use as bait."

I was taken aback. "Excuse me?"

"Ok, bait is not really the right word. But the powers that be have instructed us to wander areas where Rogue activity is high in the hopes of someone confronting us. Then we call for backup."

So I was bait, after all. Great. Way to make a girl feel useful.

"Before I was a professor, I worked with a division of the FBI, so don't worry, you're in good hands." She added.

We walked in silence for another block. We were heading straight into one of the rougher parts of downtown. The windows were barred and the lights were dim. It practically screamed crime and gang wars. I flinched at every random noise.

"Your suburbia is showing," Professor McTavish chuckled.

I laughed to hide my embarrassment.

Suddenly, someone turned out of the alley and stopped in the middle of the sidewalk. She was dressed in black with her long blond hair pulled into a high ponytail.

"Agent Thompson?" I gasped, stopping mid-step. She looked exactly like I remembered:

Serious, cold, and chic in that corporate-bad-bitch kind of way.

The woman smirked. "Ah, little Bianca, we meet again. How are your parents doing?"

I gritted my teeth. "Don't talk about them," I hissed. "It's because of you that I can't have a normal conversation with them. They're so brainwashed it's pathetic."

"I do what I have to do to keep our kind secret," Agent Thompson replied. "It's my job."

"You keep using that line and I'm going to stop believing it." I spat.

Professor McTavish stepped between us. "What's going on? You know her?"

Agent Thompson's eyes lit up. "Well if it isn't Siobhan. How's civilian life serving you?" She sneered.

I looked back and forth between the two women.

"I heard you vanished." Siobhan didn't answer her question. Her hands were visibly shaking.

"What would you care?" Agent Thompson snapped. "It's not like you've seen me since you turned your back on the FBI."

"I didn't turn my back on anyone!" Siobhan shouted.

Agent Thompson held up her hand. "Please, let's not get into this in front of the child." She gestured to me. "Grown up matters will have to wait. You're not why I'm here, Siobhan."

I glared at her. "What do you want with me?" If it was a fight she wanted, I'd happily give it to her after what she did to my parents and tried to do to Daniel. This woman was just a little too keen on brainwashing people for my liking. I flexed my fingers, feeling my psychic energy building up.

"I've come to collect you, my dear. You've evaded capture too many times. The others aren't as powerful as you. You're the one my master needs." Agent Thompson grinned.

I braced myself. "You traitor!" I shouted. "You've gone Rogue!"

Agent Thompson clapped sarcastically. "And you're a smart girl. I'd give you a cookie if I had one."

Professor McTavish reached for her phone.

"I wouldn't do that if I were you." Agent Thompson said. She locked eyes with her and the energy around them pulsed.

Siobhan slowly let the cell phone fall from her hand. She stared back silently, her eyes were blank and cold.

"Stop that!" I shrieked.

Siobhan crumpled to the ground and lay still.

"What did you do to her?" I screamed.

"Oh, she'll be fine." Agent Thompson said with a shake of her head. "I wanted some privacy. I'm sure you've realized by now that I can be very persuasive." She grinned. "Now, come with me."

I felt her psychic energy surge towards me and forced my mental blocks as high as they would go. I could not let her enter my mind. If I did, who knew what she might brainwash me into doing. "Fuck off!" I screamed. I used my energy to latch onto a discarded soda can and threw it at her.

Our connection was cut off as she dodged. "You've improved since I saw you last. Excellent work, Bianca. My master will be most pleased with your progress."

"I'm not going anywhere with you." I spat.

Agent Thompson snickered. "I'm sorry my dear, but you don't have a choice in the matter."

Remembering Ryland's advice, I looked down, following her movements with only my peripheral vision. Most telepathic people had to use eye contact to get what they wanted. If I could fight her without looking at her directly, I'd have a chance.

I heard footsteps approaching fast. "Stop where you are!" An authoritative voice boomed. "Put your hands up where I can see them." A cop. I was saved.

Agent Thompson swore under her breath. "Now is not the time for this," She said to the officer.

"Don't look her in the eye!" I shouted, praying they'd take my advice.

"Hands where I can see them!" The cop shouted again.

I raised my hands. Agent Thompson was backing away now. If she escaped, we might lose our only lead on these Rogues. I couldn't let that happen. I twitched my fingers and pulled my tracker from my belt loop. With my energy, I latched the tracker onto the back of her jacket. It was small enough that she might not notice it until it was too late. She would run back to wherever she was hiding and then we might have a chance at stopping these Rogues. But, for my plan to work she needed to escape.

"Tell your master that I'll never come quietly!" I shouted, using my mind to push her backwards into the alley.

The cop and his partner ran into the scene, their guns drawn. One tackled me to the ground and shouted something into his radio.

The other came back from the alley empty handed. "She got away," He said. "Just gone. Like she disappeared."

Professor McTavish groaned as she regained consciousness. She startled, bolting upright with two guns in her face. "Whoa, officers," She said and held up her hands. "Code Silver."

The officers lowered their weapons. "Let's see your ID."

Siobhan presented an identification card.

"That checks out," The taller officer said. He gestured for the his partner to let me go.

I struggled to my feet. My cheek was burning where it hit the pavement.

"We weren't notified of psychic training in this area today," The other cop said. He shoved his gun into the holster and crossed his arms over his chest.

"Apologies," Siobhan said. She went to my side and put a hand on my shoulder. "The academy has been investigating along side the FBI, so it was a need to know basis."

"Need to know basis," The cop spoke over her. "Figures." He shook his head and gestured down the alley. "Your little friend got away."

"Shit," Siobhan sighed. "I let her get into my head. Are you ok, Bianca?" She asked.

"Been better." I wiped the blood from my cheek.

The cops retreated back to their cruiser and left without another word.

"Aren't they going to investigate this?" I muttered.

"Out of their jurisdiction, I'd imagine. Other public servants let us psychics deal with our own problems more times than not. " Siobhan explained. "Honestly, it's for the best. Could you imagine what might happen in a psychic versus rookie cop showdown? I'd rather not." She shuddered.

I nodded and wiped my hands on my pants. They were scratched and bloody, too. "It doesn't matter, because I know where she's headed."

"What? How?" Professor McTavish asked in disbelief.

I pointed to my belt loop where the tracker used to be. "Easy as pie. Now all we need to do is track her."

CHAPTER TWENTY THREE

"I am both impressed and terrified, Miss Bianca," Ms. Blackwell said.

Siobhan and I teleported straight back to the academy and woke the Major and Ms. Blackwell. The Major was still dressed in his pajamas with a burgundy house coat thrown over top. Ms. Blackwell was never seen looking less than perfect, so she had changed for the occasion, heels and all.

The resident IT guy was typing away like a madman on the computer. His office was dark and not meant for the crowd of us who had squeezed in. He seemed mildly annoyed at this late-night tracking session interrupting his gaming time. A Nintendo console was still on, paused mid-battle.

"Are you sure it was her?" The Major asked.

Siobhan nodded. "Of course, it was. I just can't believe one of our own would do this. I went to the academy with her. We went through basic training together. Started with the FBI the same day." Her voice cracked.

So that was how they knew each other. I realized how devastating it would have been for Professor McTavish. The emotional hurt would have weakened her mind enough to make manipulation as easy as opening a door.

The Major's face was like stone. "Another Rogue who knows our secrets." He muttered.

"At least Bianca's quick thinking will help us track her," Ms. Blackwell said and beamed at me.

"Got it," The IT guy said. A large monitor showed a map of Detroit, with about half a dozen dots blinking in random areas, indicating wherever a teleporter was.

"Great." Siobhan leaned over the desk. "Her tracking code was B4048-A." She rattled off the number.

The IT guy typed it into the search and punched the enter button with an unnecessary flourish. He leaned back in his ergonomic chair while the computer screen flashed. The map zoomed into an industrial area a few miles west of the academy.

"It's still moving," Siobhan said.

Everyone else leaned in to watch the little yellow dot on the screen. It vanished and reappeared on a small island in the river.

"What?" Siobhan exclaimed. "Thompson can't teleport."

"Apparently someone who can teleport was helping her." The Major said. "That island is a natural reserve for plants and animals. Why would they be going there?" He touched the screen. The yellow dot was steady and unmoving.

The IT guy wiped the screen with a cloth and went back to typing furiously.

"Alright, good job everyone." The Major wrote the coordinates on a slip of paper. "I'm going to notify the FBI at once. Everyone else, you can go to bed."

I groaned as I forced myself from the chair. My head was throbbing, and my body was begging for a long hot shower.

I said goodbye to the professors and made my way to the dorms. My bed was calling my name and I couldn't wait to sleep. It was all I could do to drag myself to the washrooms to shower before returning to my room.

Just as I was opening my door, I heard footsteps. I looked up and saw Ryland. He was dressed in loose sweatpants and a white t-shirt. His hair was damp and tousled. "Ryland, what are you doing up?"

"Late night gym sesh, you know how it is." He shrugged. "Plus, I couldn't sleep. I was wondering how your first night in the field went." He glanced at my cheek, noticing the graze from the pavement. "What happened?"

I almost replied before shutting my mouth with a snap. "Why don't you come into my room? We shouldn't talk about it here."

Ryland grinned mischievously and took a seat on my bed while I combed my damp hair.

He looked utterly delicious in casual clothes, leaning back against a pile of pillows.

I told him what happened as best as I could remember, from the moment we left to the moment we got back. He sat there with his eyes wide, taking it all in silently. I found myself strangely calm as I recounted the evening.

I finished applying my face cream and turned off the light, leaving the room with a shadowy glow from the moon shining through the window. "At least I thought to use the tracker. The FBI will be notified of their location and that's that. Now we can finally stop worrying about the Rogues."

Ryland inched over so I could lay down beside him. He brought the blankets up to my chest and cradled me in one arm. "I wish that were true, Bianca."

"What do you mean?" I asked.

"Even if they catch those Rogues, more will take their place. There's enough psychic people out there that disagree with the government to keep the sentiment going." He explained. "I've been part of this world since I was born and I can't remember a time that someone wasn't trying to shake things up."

"That's not very reassuring," I said as I nestled into the crook of his arm. I struggled to keep my eyes open.

"Don't worry about it tonight. I'm sure everything will work out." Ryland kissed my forehead and held me until I fell asleep.

The next day passed in a suspiciously normal fashion. Breakfast, classes, and training all went on as usual. It wasn't until after training that Ms. Blackwell motioned for me to stay back and speak to her.

Once my classmates had left, Ms. Blackwell smiled at me. She never showed her true feelings to the class. "I wanted to thank you again for your fine work yesterday," She said. "If it wasn't for you, things could have turned out horribly for everyone."

I shrugged modestly. "I just had an idea and followed through. Have the Rogues been found?"

Ms. Blackwell hushed me and looked around. "We shouldn't say that too loudly, Miss Bianca. All I know is that the powers that be are working on it and we need to carry on as before. I promise I will let you know more if I can."

An alarm started sounding. The beeps were rapid and loud.

I groaned and put my hands over my ears. "What is that?" I shouted over the noise.

"Looks like it's time for me to let you know more." Ms Blackwell said with a shake of her head. "Come, follow me."

She walked off at such a speed I struggled to keep up with her. How she walked and fought in stiletto heels was beyond me. We stopped at a door near the Major's office. It was unmarked and I hand always assumed it was a janitor's closet.

Ms. Blackwell knocked a specific rhythm on the door, and it opened a few seconds later.

This was no janitor's closet. Instead, it was a boardroom with seating for about twenty people, computer screens on the walls and another screen built into the table. The lights were dim. A dozen students were sitting at the long table accompanied by Major Griffiths, Professor McTavish and a few others I didn't know the names of.

"Holy shit," I said, unable to control myself.

Ms Blackwell nudged me forward and closed the door behind us. The muffled sound of the alarm stopped abruptly as she hit a button on the wall.

"So, we're all here then." The Major looked up from the screen on the table and his eyes widened. "Ms. Blackwell, Bianca is not part of the student task force."

I stiffened, noticing Ryland and Luke at the back of the room. They both looked as surprised to see me as everyone else. "Student task force?" I repeated.

Ms. Blackwell stepped in front of me. "I think she'll do just fine. She's the reason we know where the Rogues are, she deserves to be here."

"The FBI called for backup because the situation is dire. This is not a field trip." The Major said, his face turning red.

Professor McTavish stood up. "Give her a chance!"

I stood awkwardly as the teachers fought amongst themselves.

The Major sighed and raised his hands for silence. "Bianca, this is a serious mission. There is a real risk of danger and injury. My colleagues seem to think you are ready and I'm willing to give you a chance. The most important question is: do you want to join us?"

I looked around the room and my eyes locked with Ryland. He gave me a reassuring smile and a discrete thumbs up. "I do." I said firmly.

In the next hour that followed I learned what the student task force was. The top students from the academy volunteered as reserve agents for the local FBI branches in situations where more manpower was needed. It was on a volunteer basis and only the best students could join.

It seemed almost surreal sitting at a table with everyone while the teachers discussed what happened. I stayed close to Ms. Blackwell, but unfortunately found myself sitting across from Zoe McMahon, who I had avoided like the plague since the competition. The bruise around her eye had faded to a dull yellow.

"The situation is dire," The Major continued. "The FBI has reason to believe that the psychic Rogues outnumber the staff on hand. They've asked for our assistance. In return, you will be rewarded for your efforts. If the situation gets too dangerous, we will pull out."

I glanced around the room. Everyone was quiet and serious.

"Any questions?" Major Griffith asked after showing us the map of the area and circling the target island.

Ryland raised his hand. "Sir, how many Rogues are we expecting?"

"It may not be the number of Rogues that matter, but their collective power. They have evaded all attempts thus far. This is our chance to grab them while they are trapped."

"What about teleporters?" Luke interjected.

"We'll deal with that when we come to it," The Major said. "I've heard rumors that the FBI has developed a device that emits distracting frequencies and makes it difficult to teleport. However, if we use them, our own agents will not be able to teleport either. I will notify the team if we have access to one."

Luke nodded and leaned back in his chair. He and Ryland exchanged glances. They were all business now. On edge and chomping at the bit, the boys were eager to get out to the front lines, I could see it burning in their eyes.

Zoe raised her hand. "Sir, what makes them think that we have any chance against them if their own agent are struggling?"

"Times like this call for desperate measures. Scouts have confirmed ten kidnapped youth are in the stronghold. It is not time to second-guess our abilities." The Major replied. "As always, these missions are voluntary. If anyone wishes to drop out, speak now." He held his hands behind his back, looking at each of us in turn.

No one spoke up. They were in this for the long haul. My heart pounded in my chest. I was both terrified and honored to be among them.

"Excellent. We depart before midnight. Go and prepare and we will reconvene here in three hours."

"Yes, sir." The replied echoed in the boardroom.

∞

"So this is how you guys knew about all this gear," I said, leaning against the door of the supply closet.

Ryland tossed me a pair of night-vision goggles. "Hey, we would have told you the truth if we could." He jumped down from the ladder with a fully prepped backpack of supplies and hooked it over his shoulder.

I couldn't stop myself from smiling. I slipped the goggles onto my utility belt. The uniform was the same as the off-site training outfit I wore last night, except we had a reflective red band stitched on our belt to distinguish us from the fully fledged agents.

Luke came around the corner with more gear. "Tell me how we got stuck with prepping the bags again?" The bags were heavy but designed to take up as little space as possible.

"To show me how it's done," I replied with a smile.

"I thought we were done babysitting you." Luke teased.

I punched him in the shoulder gently. "You know you love it." I laughed. "I'm totally stoked to be going out on a real mission with you guys."

Ryland's grin faltered. "We are too, but please be careful. This isn't school. It's real life. People might get hurt," He said.

"I'll be fine." I promised. I had no doubt that I could take anything the Rogues sent my way now that I was better trained in combat and psychic defense. These assholes had kidnapped my friend and now they were kidnapping psychic teens all over the city. They had to be stopped and I would not sit on the sidelines to watch the action.

"Are we packed?" Ms. Blackwell said. The sounds of her heels on the tiled floor announced her presence before her voice. She inspected the bags briefly, checking that everything was in its place.

"Yes," Luke said. "Checked them all myself."

"Alright, let's get going then," She said, picking up four of the bags and walking out with her heels echoing with every step.

"She's so cool," I said wistfully.

Ryland and Luke chuckled. "Don't go getting a crush on the prof now," Ryland added.

"What? No way!" I shouldered two more bags. "Haven't you guys have heard of woman crushes? Geez, not everything has to be about physical attraction." I stomped off down the hall, not waiting for them to catch up.

I lined up the bags against the wall. Everyone had changed into their tactical clothes, including Professor McTavish and the other professor who I didn't know. The Major would stay back with the surveillance team to control communication between both parties.

"I hope you packed those bags right," Zoe hissed under her breath as she walked by.

I bit back my angry retort and shook the tension from my shoulders. Now was not the time for fighting, especially if she needed to walk. I'd deal with her later.

"Actually, I packed them." Luke cut in. He must have heard her.

Zoe looked away and busied herself with her reflective belt.

Ryland dropped the last few bags against the wall and adjusted his t-shirt that had ridden up as he walked. "That's the last of the gear," He said.

I caught the smallest glimpse of his abs and felt my thighs tremble. I would need serious bedroom therapy once this was all over. Nothing like a hot man to de-stress and take my worries away for the night.

The team put on their trackers and bags, lined up and then waited for instruction. I stood between Luke and Ryland, not sure if I should be scared or excited. I looked up at Ryland and caught his eye.

"Don't worry, I'll be looking out for you," He said.

"I'm not scared." My voice sounded braver than my heart.

Ryland smiled as if he knew I was lying. "It's ok to be nervous," He said.

"We will leave from the teleportation point. The agents have set up a temporary camp outside the Rogue territory. I have the coordinates to get everyone there safely. We will need to make two trips in order to take everyone over. Professor McTavish and I will help out with the transportation of other students." She walked back and forth as she spoke.

Ryland touched my hand and knitted his fingers between mine. A feeling of reassurance surged through me when we held hands.

Once the instructions were complete, we filed out of the building and towards the teleportation point. We didn't encounter a single other student as we walked. The lights in the dorm were almost all dark. The moon shone above, casting long shadows behind us.

"You're the only student who can teleport on the team?" I asked Luke as he reviewed the coordinates.

"Yes," He said.

"Doesn't that put us at a disadvantage. We can't move as quick." My voice trailed off.

"I prefer not to take more than two students at a time," He said. "But in an emergency, I think I could do four." He shook his head and pocketed the location that was scribbled on a piece of paper. "I'd rather not think about it, though."

I nodded.

"Ok, first group, let's go." Professor McTavish called out. Zoe and another guy stepped forward. She took them by the hands and vanished.

"Next!" Ms. Blackwell called out and motioned to Luke.

I said a little prayer as Luke took my hand. In a pop and a flash, we were gone.

CHAPTER TWENTY FOUR

We reappeared in a parking lot. There were trucks and trailers parked around us and the area was buzzing with activity. Agents were everywhere. I caught a glimpse of Siobhan as she teleported back to the academy for the next group of students.

Ryland shook his head and leaned against the trailer. "God I hate that," He grumbled.

"I think I'm getting used to it," I said with a laugh.

"Still better than getting sick on a plane," Luke said and handed me his bag. "I'll be right back." He vanished.

Zoe and the other student were waiting nearby. An FBI agent in uniform approached us with a clipboard. "I take it you are the students from the academy?" He asked.

We all nodded.

The agent scribbled something on his notepad and walked away.

"Geez, thanks for the warm welcome," Ryland muttered sarcastically. "We're just risking our necks out here to help, no big deal."

Ms. Blackwell appeared with two more students and left as quickly as she came.

Once everyone had been teleported safely, the teachers left to meet with the agents and get filled in on what had happened since the SOS call went out. We had nothing else to do but wait.

One trailer had been set up as a temporary lounge with coffee and snacks. My appetite was overpowered by my nerves, so I just sat with a cup of coffee in my hands. Everyone was quiet and focused on their own thoughts. Ryland rubbed my knee as he stared at the floor.

We didn't have to wait long for Ms. Blackwell to come back with instructions. We all flinched at the sound of the door banging shut.

"Ok, everyone, gather around. We've been given our instructions. The main force will teleport to the island in half an hour. We are to follow behind them and stay hidden for support if it's needed. We have a team of thirty psychic agents armed to the teeth, so if all goes well, we won't need to take any action at all."

"And if it doesn't?" Someone asked.

There was a long pause. Ms. Blackwell cleared her throat. "Then we'll deal with that if and when we get there," She said. -

The seriousness of the situation hit me. This was a real mission with real risks. I glanced at the students standing around me, none of them looked scared. I wondered how many of them were as nervous as I was behind their poker faces.

A man entered the trailer. He practically radiated with authority. His uniform was crisp and his mustache was so straight someone could use it as a ruler. He cleared his throat and the room silenced. "Good evening, students," He said. "Ms Blackwell, thank you for collecting some back up so quickly. Please send my regards to the Major."

Ms. Blackwell nodded and introduced him. "Everyone this is Agent Radcliffe. He oversees all the FBI's involvement with Rogue activity. Tonight, you answer to him."

We nodded in unison. My hands were trembling again. I did my best to keep them still at my sides.

"Very good," He said. Agent Radcliffe took a small device from his back pocket.

It was a foldable tablet; I'd never seen one before and had to hold in a gasp as he unfolded it. It was incredibly thin and sleek, nothing like my mom's iPad at home.

A map loaded onto the screen. "The Rogues have made a temporary stronghold on this island. There are no proper roads or bridges to lead to it. It is marked as a wildlife reserve, which is likely how they went undetected for so long." He explained. "The island is large enough that we will have to split into groups to cover the ground. The Rogues are using an old research building for shelter. We have every reason to assume they are armed, dangerous, and will not hesitate to harm the youth they have kidnapped."

I swallowed hard. My mouth was dry and my throat felt prickly.

He began shouting off names. "Hernandez, Williams, McMahon, you'll be with delta team. As is the protocol, all student teams need a supervisor. Blackwell will accompany you."

I breathed a sigh of relief, at least I'd have Ryland with me. Too bad Zoe would be there, but someone as powerful as her might come in handy, if I could survive her constant glares.

Ms. Blackwell ushered us out of the trailer as Agent Radcliffe continued breaking students off into groups. "We'll wait here for the rest of the team," She said.

Ryland was bouncing from one foot to another. He was the most eager person in the group. "I'm ready," He said.

Ms. Blackwell shot him a look. "Agents go in first, Mr. Williams," She warned. "We're back up only. I don't need to remind you of that, do I?"

Ryland frowned. "No, ma'am." He lived for action and craved battle.

I hoped some of his energy would wear off on me before we headed out.

A small group of agents in black uniforms approached us. I assumed they were the delta team that Agent Radcliffe mentioned. They spoke to Ms. Blackwell quietly before pulling their face masks up.

"We're ready to go, team," Ms. Blackwell said.

Ryland pulled his face mask up and I followed suit. My heart was pounding so hard I thought it might break through my chest.

Ms. Blackwell checked the coordinates and we teleported out of the base camp.

We landed in the middle of a forest. The ground was muddy and the trees blocked out the light of the moon. There were no sounds around us. The delta team appeared a moment later. They had two teleporters bring in all ten of them, which was more than impressive.

Our small student group hung back while the agents went to work. Ryland nudged me and slid his night vision goggles over his eyes. I took the hint and unclipped mine from my belt. Once they were on, I could see clearly again.

I watched the agents disappear into the night. They moved swiftly and silently like shadows. I waited impatiently, fidgeting and moving from one foot to the other.

Zoe shot me yet another glare. "Hey, chill out." She hissed.

I crouched down and forced myself to keep still. A moment later, I felt a strange pull in my chest. The feeling was calling to me. It was loud and intense. I put a hand to my chest, trying to calm my nerves.

"Are you ok?" Ryland asked.

I swallowed hard. "I think so. I just feel it."

"Feel what?"

"There's an intense energy pulling towards me. It was the same as last time and the same feeling the first day my powers emerged." I tried to keep the panic from my voice. "It's stronger now. It feels angry somehow."

Ryland stared at me for a moment.

"You must think I'm crazy," I said quickly.

"No," Ryland said. "Just worried about you. Are you sure you're up for this?"

His question only strengthened my resolve. "Yes." I looked back out into the darkness. There was no sign of the agents or anything at all for that matter. Darkness stared back at me through the trees.

The feeling in my chest grew stronger. It was pulling me like a magnet. I held my breath and ignored it. I didn't need anyone to think I was weak or scared.

"Bianca." A voice rang through my head.

I forced myself not to panic. It was the same voice that I heard during the last battle. The voice of the floating woman. What did she want with me?

A bright light flashed in the distance.

Ms. Blackwell snapped to attention. "It's beginning," She said. "Stay low and stay quiet."

Zoe whimpered.

I didn't bother glaring at her. I had no time to be drawn into her negativity. The pulling feeling felt as if it was tearing my chest in two. I dropped to a knee, pressing my hand against my chest.

The walkie-talkie on Ms. Blackwell's hip crackled with static. Someone said something that I couldn't make out over the feedback.

"Bianca. What are you doing here?"

I tucked my head down, wishing the voice would get out of my head. I gritted my teeth and counted down from ten. This was not the time to panic.

The sound of a twig snapping behind us broke through the silence. Ms. Blackwell turned around first and she was thrown to the ground by an invisible force. She didn't move.

Two Rogues emerged from the bushes and lashed out with telekinetic energy, freezing us where we stood.

I strained against the force but was unable to move an inch. I gasped for air as they squeezed us.

"Looks like we found the little bird that master has been asking for," One of the Rogues snickered. His face was concealed with a black mask.

His partner nodded and let out a shrill whistle.

Ryland groaned, pushing forward inch by inch, trying to gain traction on the muddy bed of leaves beneath us.

"Ah, ah," The first one threw his hand forward and locked his power onto Ryland. "Don't get any bright ideas."

Zoe fainted beside me and fell to the ground.

I didn't have time to worry about her. The masked woman appeared between her two Rogue grunts. She hovered in a long white dress, barefoot, in an oddly calming sort of way. "There you are, Bianca."

The woman snapped her fingers and the Rogue released me from his telekinetic grip. "We don't need to be using force like that on her." She said, her silent voice pushing into everyone's head.

I couldn't speak. Tears were leaking from my eyes. I tore my night vision goggles from my face.

Ryland winced and looked away.

"Don't worry, boy, I'm not here to hurt anyone." The masked woman continued.

Ms. Blackwell groaned from where she lay on the ground.

I coughed to cover up the noise. She was the only one here strong enough to take them on. She needed to wake up and fast. "What do you want with us?" I asked, staring at the masked woman.

The woman spoke in our heads. "I have come for you, Bianca."

"Me? Why?" I demanded. "What the hell makes me so special that you're willing to hurt people over it?"

The woman chuckled. The sound echoed in my mind. "Oh my dear, they haven't told you, have they?"

"What?" I asked. "Who hasn't told me what?"

If it were possible for a blank white mask to look smug, now was the time. "They haven't told you that you're my daughter?"

CHAPTER TWENTY FIVE

"Your daughter?" I shrieked.

Ms. Blackwell groaned and wrapped her hand around my ankle. The energy trembled around us and we teleported.

I landed on my ass and rolled against the fence. "What the hell?" We were back at the academy. "What the hell!" I jumped to my feet.

Ms. Blackwell stood and dusted off her clothes. "I'm sorry Bianca," She said.

"No. Send me back! Bring me back!" I screamed. "That woman! That woman is my mother?" My words failed me as I was overcome with confusion and grief. I fell to my knees, choking back my sobs.

"I'm sorry," Ms. Blackwell repeated. "If I would have known, I wouldn't have brought you."

Anger surged through me. How did that make it any better? "Bring me back!" I growled.

"I can't do that. You're not in the right mind to be fighting right now."

Her calm voice infuriated me. I jumped up again and forced my energy towards her.

Ms. Blackwell batted my psychic hold away as if it were a fly. "I believe you just proved my point."

I let my hands fall to my sides and the psychic energy receded back to my spine. I let out a long sigh and wiped my tears. "I just can't believe it," I whispered.

"I don't know what to tell you," Ms. Blackwell said. "Come with me. Maybe the Major will have some answers."

We walked in silence to the main building. The Major was holed up in the boardroom with two other teachers. A two-way radio was at the center of the table and maps were transmitted on the screens. Yellow dots moved about the map, one for every student with a tracker.

"Sir, there's been an incident." Ms. Blackwell said as she slammed the door.

The Major's eyebrows shot up. "What? What happened? Are the students all accounted for?"

Ms. Blackwell gestured to me. "I believe someone has been keeping something from us."

The major looked from me to Ms. Blackwell and sighed. He sunk back in his chair and rubbed his temples with his short fingers. "I see."

I stomped up to the table and slammed my fist down on the wood. "The Rogue leader is my mother." It wasn't a question; the rage gave my voice an edge.

Major Griffiths didn't flinch. "Well, that is a surprise," He said.

"So you didn't know the identity of my mother?" I asked.

"Oh, no, I did. But I didn't know she was involved with these Rogues." He knitted his fingers together and rested his chin on them. "Interesting."

"Interesting?" I echoed. "That's all you have to say? You knew the identity of my birth mother and didn't tell me?"

"I believe you were the one who told me that Mr. and Mrs. Hernandez were all the family you needed." Major Griffiths replied.

It took all of my strength not to wipe the smirk off his face. "How dare you," I said. "How dare you keep this secret from me!"

"Why do you think we wanted to secure you as a student so badly? Why do you think I asked Ms. Blackwell to personally teach you, when she normally only mentors graduating students? If you're as powerful as your birth mother, well, I needed to make sure all controls were in place."

My jaw dropped.

"I'm not the enemy, Bianca. I assure you I meant no harm. But, it is my job to protect all young psychics from the world and from themselves. I had no choice."

My legs gave out and I grasped the table to keep myself upright. I stared down at the wood grain. "My mother. Someone knew. Someone knew this whole time."

"If she is involved, I'm afraid the students need to fall back. This is not the battle we planned for." The Major motioned to Ms. Blackwell. "I will notify the agents. You need to return for our students."

"What about me?" I demanded.

"You will stay put, young lady. We cannot have you compromising this mission. We'll deal with the rest later." The Major said and swiveled in his chair; the phone already pressed to his ear.

That was the signal that the conversation was over. My shoulders slumped.

Ms. Blackwell touched my shoulder gently.

I flinched away. "Don't touch me." I took a deep breath and wiped my tears away. Grabbing the door handle, I took one last look around the room and at the back of the head of the man who had broken my trust beyond repair. "I need to be alone. I can't handle this right now."

"Bianca!" Ms. Blackwell called after me.

I didn't look back. The door slammed behind me and my footsteps echoed down the hall. It was dark and empty, a fitting description of how I felt. I came to a stop in the middle of the hall. I didn't know what to do or where to go. Did I go back to the dorms? Did I call Daniel? What about my parents? I was numb.

I started walking again, letting my feet lead me down the familiar path towards the training facility. When I entered the empty training room my numbness faded away and furious buzzing replaced it. Energy began coursing through me, threatening to break out.

I let it out. I screamed at the top of my lungs, throwing up my arms and grasping everything I could reach with my psychic connection. Stacks of mats, weights, and balls came crashing to the ground. The racks and shelves came next. The rattling metal echoed; the sound amplified by the tall ceiling.

It wasn't enough. I grabbed a few rubber balls and tore them in half. It came easier than anything that I had learned in class. I threw the balls back down and ran my fingers through my hair. My fingers got caught in the elastic, so I ripped it out.

How could have people known who my mother was and not told me? My adoptive parents always said that the records were lost. There was no trace of my birth mother. She just disappeared.

My chest began to hurt again. This stress might give me a heart attack if I didn't get my emotions under control. I took a long breath in and out.

The Rogue woman who had hurt so many people, including me and my friends, was my mother? Why now? Why her? I had lived my entire life not knowing who put me up for adoption and I had always accepted my adoptive parents. Blood didn't make someone family, especially if that blood abandoned you as a child.

I kicked open the back door of the training facility to let in some cool air. The breeze hit my sweaty skin and took my breath away. I stopped for a moment just to enjoy the stillness of the night. The stars were visible for once, without a single cloud to obscure them. The grass waved back and forth, and the breeze rolled through the academy grounds. One of the lights atop the fence was flickering off and on in a slow rhythm.

I took a deep breath of the cool air and let the sensation wash over me. My heart slowed to its normal pace and my hands stopped shaking.

My mother was out there this whole time. What a strange thought. I had lived eighteen years without thinking twice about her and yet I had just seen her face to face. Well, face to mask, I guess. Why hadn't anyone told me? Why hadn't she come for me sooner? Why was she a Rogue of all things? Just my luck, I finally met my birth mother and she was probably getting arrested this second.

I rubbed my arms and crossed them over my chest. The empty feeling in my chest wouldn't let up. I knew what I had to do. I had to go back to Major Griffiths and demand to meet her. I could not let this chance of knowing my birth mother slip away, even if she was a criminal.

"Hurry! We need to get to the coordinates. An SOS has gone out. The agents need to pull back!" Someone shouted.

"I don't give a shit about the agents; our students are out there!" Ms. Blackwell's voice came next.

I saw Ms. Blackwell and another teacher running to the teleportation point as fast as they could.

"What the hell?" I thought out loud. I watched them dash to the teleportation point and disappear in a flash.

I ran out of the training facility and towards the teleportation point before I could talk myself out of it. The students were in trouble. Ryland, Luke, even stuck-up Zoe. They were in danger because of me. If I hadn't gone, Ms. Blackwell would have been there.

I skidded to a stop at the gate. What was I going to do now? Wait for them to get back? I glanced around and saw no one. I shivered and swept my hair away from my face. I wasn't out of ideas yet. I looked over my shoulder one last time before slipping into the teleportation area.

There was one option left. I didn't know if it was even possible, but I had to try. I stepped into the middle of the sandy teleportation area and closed my eyes. I centered my mind and then reached out with my energy. After a moment, I began to see spots of light in the dark, marking the energy signatures of students who had teleported recently. Most were dull and barely visible, thankfully one shined brightly.

I opened my eyes and knelt down beside Ms. Blackwell's energy signature. It was invisible to the naked eye, but I could feel it in my mind. "You're crazy, Bianca," I said to myself. Could this really be possible? There was only one way to find out.

"Please work!" I held my breath, planted my hand on the pulsing energy signature, and hoped for a miracle.

CHAPTER TWENTY SIX

When I opened my eyes, I was in the middle of a forest. I gasped, unable to believe that it wasn't my imagination. I bolted to my feet and looked around. Yep, this was it, the conversation area.

"Holy shit!" I breathed. "Yes! I did it!" I barely contained my excited screams. I didn't think it was possible, but here I was. I hijacked the energy signature entirely on my own. It was too good to be true.

Once I caught my breath, I backed against a tree to get a good look at my surroundings. I lost my night vision goggles and my backpack during the confusion last time; I had nothing but a pair of gloves and a tiny flashlight in my pocket.

I plucked my tracker off my belt loop and tossed it on the ground. I didn't need anyone interfering this time. No more saving me for my own good. I could handle this myself.

With the help of the pathetic beam from the tiny flashlight, I navigated through the trees and bushes until I found what looked to be an over-grown dirt path. The indents in the road were narrower than a car, a four-wheeler maybe? They said this used to be a research facility, so that path probably went directly to the building the Rogues were using as a hideout.

Keeping the flashlight on the ground, I made my way down the path in what I could only hope was the right direction.

After what was probably only a few minutes, I could hear sounds of other people in the distance. Someone was shouting orders, but I couldn't make them out. I continued to follow the path, hoping the voices would get louder. I hesitated when I heard a gunshot but pressed forward.

"No time to chicken out now," I whispered to myself. My only way home would be to find the agents, help them take down the Rogues, and hopefully not have to explain how I got myself back here. Hopefully, if they realized how useful I was, they'd overlook yet another instance of insubordination on my part.

The unkempt dirt road began to widen, and I could see lights in the distance. A small building came into view. It was square and made of cement bricks, with two floors and many broken windows. The abandoned research building.

I stopped at the rear of the building. I could hear the agents not too far off, probably attacking at the front. There was no guard posted at the back door.

"Bianca? Bianca!" Someone hissed.

I whirled around, my power surging. "Who's there?"

It was Zoe, Ryland, and Luke. They were hiding in the bushes at the edge of the path.

My arms fell to my sides. "Oh, thank goodness you're ok!"

Ryland grinned. "I should say the same for you. We got separated during a scuffle."

I crouched down beside them in the dark. "How did you escape?"

"The Rogues vanished after you did." Ryland said and then paled. "Wait. How did you get back here? Did you hear what that mask lady said?"

"It's a long story, and yeah I did." I brushed off the topic of my teleportation hijack to focus on the more important matter. "She said she was my mother."

Luke gasped. "So, it's true!"

"I told you," Zoe snapped. "So what are you doing back here? How can we trust you if this Rogue is your mom?"

Ryland and Luke glared at her.

"You don't have to trust me," I said before either of the boys could come to my defense. "But I did come back to help, so you can either come with us or stay here."

Zoe shrunk back at my tone. "Ok."

"So, what's the plan?" I asked Ryland. "Or, what was the plan before I interrupted you?"

Ryland nodded to the back of the building. "The agents have the Rogues distracted at the front and they've left the back door unmanned. We are going to get in there and save the hostages."

"All of them?" I asked.

"I'll teleport them to the agent base camp." Luke said. "It'll take a few trips but that's all we got. Once the hostages are secure, then the agents can do their work without having to worry about those kids."

I nodded. I wanted to ask if they had seen the masked woman, but I didn't need to give anyone a reason to doubt me.

"Once we get the kids out safely, Luke will teleport us back to the camp. We're not to go head to head with the Rogues under any circumstances." Ryland added. "Let's all get back safe in one piece, alright?"

Everyone nodded.

Ryland was in his element, a natural-born warrior and an inspiring leader. I felt my chest go tight watching him prepare for the mission. He was so ready for this. I felt safe just having him around.

"So are we teleporting into the research building?" Zoe asked.

Luke shook his head. "Nope, we're going to do this the old-fashioned way."

Ryland lead us to the abandoned building. A strange energy flowed around the building that made me feel dizzy. If anyone else noticed it, they said nothing.

Ryland pulled on the door, but it was rusted and wouldn't budge. "Bianca, would you do the honors?"

I grinned. "Of course," I said.

Zoe rolled her eyes.

I ignored her and grabbed the door with my psychic energy. With one hard pull, the handle snapped off, and the door swung inward, hanging crooked off the hinges. It took all my effort to not look back at Zoe to see the expression on her face.

Ryland peered into the darkness. "There's no sign of anyone," He said and motioned for us to follow him.

I couldn't use my flashlight, so I settled with waiting for my eyes to adjust to the darkness and following the shadowy outline of Ryland through the building. The entire back room was empty except for some old boxes and tables.

"It's a walk-out basement," Luke said. "We need to get upstairs."

We stopped at the stairs to listen for sounds of anyone above us. The agents had them distracted and outside, so the likelihood of anyone in the house was slim. We had to hope that we could overpower whoever had been left behind to watch the kidnapped teens.

"I really wish we would have been allowed some weapons," Zoe whined.

Ryland bit back a laugh. "Zoe, what's gotten into you? We are the weapons."

A shiver ran down my spine at the thought. He wasn't wrong, but I'd never want to refer to myself as a weapon. I forced those thoughts away and focused on listening for footsteps on the wooden floorboards above us.

A few minutes of complete silence satisfied Ryland and he opened the door a crack. A line of light slipped through. He paused again before opening the door a little wider. "Clear," He whispered.

The first floor was a mess. Tables were overturned, trash and food lay on the floor, the broken windows were boarded up, and graffiti was sprayed over the walls. It looked barely inhabitable.

I wrinkled my nose at the smell. "Come on, let's get upstairs." I whispered.

Ryland nodded. We slipped around the corner and went up the next flight of stairs.

More shouts and gunfire erupted from somewhere outside. I blocked out the noise and focused on the task at hand.

The door at the top of the stairs was locked. I made short work of it with another telekinetic trick. We paused before opening the door.

The top floor was just as much of a mess as the bottom floor. Ten cots were lined up against the wall, each with a young teen, somewhere between the ages of twelve and sixteen sitting on them. They were sleeping with one wrist handcuffed to the bed so they couldn't escape.

My heart fell to the pit of my stomach. "Oh my god," I said.

"Who would do this?" Zoe echoed my feelings.

The boys didn't stop to think. "Hey, wake up, help is here."

The kids were slow to wake. They looked weak and tired. "What's going on?" The youngest girl said.

I recognized her and some of the others from the news. "We're here to get you out." I said, breaking her handcuff with my energy. Zoe glanced at me before walking to the next bed to do the same.

The room was hot and stuffy. The air conditioner in the window was plugged in but not running. I wiped sweat from my face and broke the last handcuff.

The kids sat silent and dumbfounded. I had expected a warm welcome or a thank you at the very least, but they were almost like zombies.

"How long have you been here?" I asked.

They all shrugged.

"They're probably dehydrated and in shock," Luke said. "I'll take them two at a time and they'll be safe in no time."

"You're taking us away?" A curly-haired boy said.

"We've come to save you," Luke replied and extended his hand. "Come with me and we'll get you back to your parents."

"Are you working for that woman?" One kid asked.

"No, we're the good guys." Luke said. He was trying to stay calm, but we could be caught at any moment. We needed to get these kids out while we had the chance.

"So who wants to go first?" I tried, plastering the best friendly smile I could muster. "Luke is here to take you to safety."

It was obvious from the look on their faces that none of them trusted us, which, given what they had just gone through, was to be expected.

The smallest girl raised her hand. "I'll go." Her voice trembled. She and the curly haired boy took Luke's hand.

I breathed a sigh of relief as they vanished.

The other kids gasped.

"Luke will be right back," Ryland promised. "We're all getting out together."

The younger kids crowded around the oldest, a girl who'd I'd guess to be about sixteen. She hadn't yet spoken or made eye contact with us, but I knew her face from the news. Fatima. She set his shoulders and looked at me. "We didn't think anyone was going to come for us." She said softly.

"Help is here now," I said. "No one is going to get left behind."

A minute later Luke reappeared. "Let's go quick, I have an agent standing by to retrieve them." He panted.

Two more kids raised their hands to go with him.

"Hey what's going on here?" A voice shouted. A Rogue was standing at the door, so large he nearly took up the whole frame.

I recognized him from our last fight. His nose was still crooked. How did he escape the FBI? I didn't have time to dwell on it. "Go, Luke, we got this!"

Luke grabbed the kids and teleported out before he could be stopped.

I held up my hands and forced my energy towards him. He fought against me with his own telekinetic powers. He was stronger than last time, probably fueled by adrenaline at the thought of the hostages getting away.

Zoe planted her feet beside me, and her powers intertwined with mine. Together we overpowered the man and threw him against the concrete wall.

"Ryland, get the kids into pairs, we'll hold him off." I shouted.

The Rogue grunted and forced himself off the wall. "Our master is not going to like this one bit," He snarled.

Luke reappeared, grabbed two more and vanished.

The man roared at us. "Those are our recruits!" He shouted, spit flying as he spoke.

Fatima stood at my other side. "You're not recruiting anyone!" Her eyes blazed.

I could see the anguish behind them. How long had she been gone from her family and kept in this disgusting hovel? My heart ached for her. "Are your psychic powers active?" I asked.

The girl nodded. "I'm just like you."

"Great," I grinned. We just had to hold off this guy long enough to get the kids out safely and then we'd be in the clear. I pushed harder with my energy and the other girl did the same.

The Rogue was stuck to the wall and unable to move. "You bitches!" He shouted and struggled against the force. Three against one was too much to handle.

Luke was panting and sweating when he teleported back in. He rubbed his eyes and reached out for the next pair.

"Just two more after this. You got this, man," Ryland said.

Luke nodded and vanished again.

"When Luke comes back, you need to go with him." I said to Fatima.

"No, I'm staying and fighting." She said, her eyes not leaving the Rogue. "I can't let them get away with taking me away. I haven't seen my family in weeks."

"I know you're angry, but there are agents out there to help us. The best thing you can do is get to safety and go with the kids." I had only been with them for a few minutes, but it was obvious they saw her as a leader, as a source of strength. "Please, you have to for them. They need you."

The girl's powers slipped, and a tear rolled down her cheek. "I'm so tired of being strong." She sniffed.

"It's ok, go with them," I said.

Luke reappeared. "Last round, let's go!"

Fatima stepped backwards, waited for one last reassuring glance from me, and then grabbed Luke's hand.

"That's all of them." Ryland shouted.

"No!" The Rogue pushed off the wall and grabbed something from his pocket. It looked like a tracker with a big button. He pushed it and an alarm rang out. "Now you're all going to pay." He fainted from exhaustion.

I let my powers adjust to a resting state. The clip in his hand was still beeping. "Turn it off!" I shouted.

Ryland stomped on it with his boot. It took a few strikes to silence it.

"What was that?" Zoe asked.

"I don't want to wait to find out." Ryland said. "Where's Luke?" The time between teleports was getting longer as he grew more tired.

The pulling energy returned to my chest and I felt faint. "Oh no," I mumbled. The energy surrounded me and filled the room. It was suffocating and the sensation was only emphasized by my realization of what was coming.

"We need to get out of here now!" I shouted.

"Why?" Ryland asked.

There was a flash of light and shadow and the masked woman appeared. "Ah, what a pleasant surprise. I see you've come back to me already, Bianca."

CHAPTER TWENTY SEVEN

The woman snapped her fingers and in a second we were transported out of the building and into the front lot. Everything around us stopped. It was like someone had paused a video game. A dome of purplish light enveloped us.

"What's going on?" I demanded. It was just me and her now, finally alone.

The woman tipped her head, her face still hidden by the mask. "I wanted to give us an opportunity to chat, my dear." Her voice was in my head.

I cringed. "Don't call me that!"

"But you're my daughter." She said.

"You may have given birth to me, but you're not my mother!" I spat. "I would never call someone who hurts innocent people my family."

"I think you might change your mind if we got to know one another." The woman said. She hovered eerily off the ground with her white dress floating just above her ankles. "I'm sure you have a lot of questions."

I hesitated. Of course, I did. What kid wouldn't? "There's nothing I need to know that is worth letting you go free," I said.

The woman laughed, and it rattled my mind. "Such brave words, coming from a girl who's just discovered her powers." The purple dome around us was fading. "I cannot pause time for much longer, my dear. You need to decide."

"Decide on what?" I asked.

"On what you will do from here, knowing what you know now." The woman gestured around us. The psychic agents and Rogues were locked in a battle, paused mid-strike, mid-shot, mid-breath. "You have the power to stop this. Come with me."

"Why me?" My voice sounded small.

"Because you are my daughter. I want to show you the truth of this world. I've been looking for you for years, my darling." The woman said.

I flinched. Had she really been looking for me? Did she really care about me, even after giving me up?

"I can read your thoughts," The woman said. "If you come with me, I will answer any question you ask." The purple flickered and the energy waned. "We don't have much time."

A psychic who could control time? Just what kind of person was she? I forced the thought away. "No, you need to face justice for your crimes. Kidnapping children? Attacking psychics? What's wrong with you?"

The psychic dome around us began to crack.

"How dare you take that tone with me," The woman hissed in my mind. "Can't you see your options are limited? If I were you, I'd think carefully." She threw up her hands and the dome evaporated. The agents and Rogues around us blinked and staggered where they stood. She held up her hands and clenched her fists. Every agent was lured into her grasp. There were about twenty of them in total, gasping for air.

"Stop it!" I screamed.

"Then choose," The woman said.

"Bianca!" Ryland, Luke, and Zoe came running out of the building. The Rogues grabbed Zoe. Two more aimed their weapons at the boys.

"Stop right there!" The woman shouted through our minds. The feeling made me dizzy and sick. The crystal that hung around her neck began to glow and the energy pulled me towards it. "Anyone move and I will have them killed."

"No!" I screamed.

Luke and Ryland exchanged a glance. Luke could teleport before a shot could be fired; Ryland wouldn't be so lucky.

"Please let them go!" I begged. "Please, you've made your point."

"Have I?" The woman echoed.

"Yes, please, don't hurt them. I'll do whatever you say."

The woman burst out in laughter, the sound reverberating through everyone's heads. "So now you'll do whatever I say. Are these precious little boys that important to you?"

"Everyone's life is valuable to me," I said.

"So young and innocent," The woman hummed. "It's adorable, really. I remember when I used to think like that. Why should I bargain with you?"

"Please, I'll do anything." I choked. "If you hurt anyone, I'll never forgive you."

"Then come with me." She held out her hand and the energy waves pulsed around us.

"No! Bianca, no!" Ryland shouted.

"Silence!" The woman flicked her wrist and tightened her psychic grip around him until his face went pale. "One more outburst like that and you're dead, boy."

I stood facing her, my hands at my sides. I didn't dare use my talents against a psychic who could make time itself stop. I took a glance at Ryland, who shook his head furiously, unable to do anything else. I took a deep breath. "If I go with you, do you promise that everyone will leave here safe and alive tonight?"

"You have my word," The woman said.

"And the Rogues will not harm them either?"

"No, your little friends and the agents are free to leave. I guarantee it," The woman said. "Being with you is more important to me than any of them." She stretched her hand out further. "Come with me and everything will make sense."

My hands trembled. I ignored Ryland's pleading look. I was doing this for their safety. To save their lives. It was my only option. I took a step forward, my shaking hand hesitating above hers.

I looked at her blank white mask, hoping to find some sliver of humanity and coming up with nothing. This was it. I had no other choice.

"Come with me, daughter." Her voice echoed in my head.

"I'm sorry!" I shouted out and took her hand. Her skin was soft and cold to the touch. The last thing I heard before we teleported was Ryland's screams.

EPILOGUE

RYLAND

Watching her teleport with that woman was the hardest thing I had ever done.

I sat in the hidden boardroom, cracking my knuckles against the table. The room was dead quiet. No one said a word. The Major was pacing back and forth. Luke had no expression. Zoe and the other few students who agreed to meet were just as shell shocked, only half of them were brave enough to show their faces at the meeting. Ms. Blackwell seemed the most distressed, tapping her fingernails on the table, her hair was a mess and her eyes were dark. She probably hadn't slept since Bianca vanished.

Neither had I.

All I could do was go to the gym to block out the pain in my heart. How could she have left us? Why did that woman take her away?

Two weeks and no word of her? Even the Rogue activity had ceased. It was as if they disappeared off the face of the earth.

The past two weeks were the longest weeks of my life. Every morning I woke up I hoped that today would be the day that Bianca would be found. I dreamed of watching her walk through the front gates completely unharmed and everything would go back to normal.

The telephone rang and everyone jumped, staring at the Major until he picked it up.

"Hello. Yes, this is Major Griffiths." He turned away from us while he spoke. There was silence. "I see. Thank you for the update." He set the receiver down and shook his head.

"So, what is it?" Luke demanded. "Any word?"

"Possibly the worst news," The Major said.

We all sucked in a collective breath.

The major tapped away on his laptop and brought up a video on the screen behind him. It was from a CC security camera, the recording was grainy, but not too distorted to hide the truth.

Bianca.

It was Bianca, flanked by two Rogues. They were breaking into a warehouse, trying to get something out of boxes. The lights flickered and the trio teleported out of sight.

How could she do this? Bianca. The most amazing, innocent, talented, caring girl I had ever met. She wouldn't be working with the

Rogues. Working for her mother? No way, it had to be a mistake. The video looped again and I knew I could not deny it. It was Bianca, there was no doubt.

Everyone sat in stunned silence.

"It seems," Major Griffiths said. "It seems that Bianca has gone Rogue."

AUTHOR'S NOTE

Thank you for reading PSYCHIC LIES (Psychic Academy Book 2). I'm so excited to share the ending of their story in the next installment of Psychic Academy. :)

If you liked PSYCHIC LIES, please consider leaving a review on Amazon or Goodreads. This helps indie authors like myself keep telling stories for readers like you!

If you're interested in getting news about upcoming releases, giveaways, book recommendations, and other great stuff, please consider subscribing to my newsletter!

NEWSLETTER : http://eepurl.com/gyMOwH

OTHER BOOKS BY SAMANTHA BELL

Psychic Academy Series

PSYCHIC SECRET (Psychic Academy 1)
PSYCHIC PRODIGY (Psychic Academy 1.5)
PSYCHIC LIES (Psychic Academy 2)
PSYCHIC TRUTH (Psychic Academy 3)

The Bloodletters Series

THE BLOODLETTERS (2019)
THE BLOOD CROWN (TBA 2020)

Stand Alone Novels

BECOMING HUMAN (2017)

ABOUT THE AUTHOR

SAMANTHA BELL is a writer, student, and self-diagnosed book hoarder. She has been living in her imagination as long as she can remember.

Support the Psychic Academy series and future projects by following Samantha Bell on social media!

FACEBOOK
https://www.facebook.com/samanthabellblog/

TWITTER
https://twitter.com/SamanthaWrites0

WEBSITE
http://www.samanthawrites.ca/

Made in the USA
Columbia, SC
20 June 2024

36307144R00169